LEGACY AND THE DOUBLE

LEGACY
AND THE
DOUBLE

CREATED BY
KOBE BRYANT

WRITTEN BY
ANNIE MATTHEW

GRANITY STUDIOS
COSTA MESA, CALIFORNIA

Dear Kobe and Gigi,
Your love, your memories and legacies
will live on forever. You left so much more
than Legacy for us. We love you and
miss you both so much.

Love you always,
Mommy, Nani, B.B., and Koko

For Kobe and Gigi
—Annie Matthew

CHAPTER ONE

THE PEDDLER

If she closed her eyes, she could still return to the moment of her victory: one month ago today, standing on center court.

Lifting her hand over her head while the crowd stood and chanted her name.

Legacy, they'd roared, stomping their feet. *LEGACY!*

But if she opened her eyes, she remembered.

That was then: back when she was a champion.

Today, Legacy Petrin was on corn porridge duty.

That meant stirring, mostly. The porridge needed to be stirred as it cooked. And stirred and stirred and stirred some more. Otherwise, it would congeal into a kind of yellow cement. Then she'd have to start all over again. The littles would be hungry and grumpy, and her father would be angry that she'd wasted the cornmeal. Even if money hadn't been quite as scarce since Legacy had brought home her tournament winnings, her father was too stubborn to change his well-ingrained habits of thrift.

So, today, instead of swinging a racket, Legacy's muscular forearms were working a long porridge spoon.

She wiped the sweat from her forehead with the sleeve of her burlap shift. Was it really possible that one month ago she'd won the nationals? It felt like a lifetime ago. No. It felt like another life altogether.

From the vantage point of where she stood now, it was hard to believe that she'd really beaten Gia. Impossible to imagine that she'd ever do it again.

Realizing this, Legacy felt a little irritation beginning to burn at the back of her throat. She should be practicing. Where were her friends? Maybe Pippa could take a turn at the cauldron.

But Pippa was probably buried under a stack of Ancient Stringing Craft tomes in the attic, seeking some kind of secret to help Legacy unlock more of her grana.

And Javi—where was he? Javi was certainly strong enough to stir this goop.

But then Legacy remembered: he'd started waking up early to head out into the woods and scrounge around for "training materials." Here at the orphanage, he was determined to train Legacy as intensely as they were able to back at the academy, with all its fancy weight-lifting machines, the whirlpools for recovery, the cafeteria full of high-protein options. So Javi spent hours gathering stones to build makeshift weight-lifting equipment, or ingredients for improvised muscle-bulk smoothies, which he strongly suggested Legacy drink before going out on her morning run, or heading into the forest for an afternoon session on court.

At the end of the day, though, the orphanage wasn't the academy.

More mornings than not, Javi came home from the woods complaining about the impossibility of training Legacy without academy equipment. And then Pippa chimed in about the shortage of stringing minerals, and how she couldn't properly re-string Legacy's racket if she didn't find a way to stock up on prosite. And once they'd gotten going, the two of them could talk all night about the absence of proper training partners for Legacy, and how she'd need to get back into shape if she was ever going to beat Gia again, and sometimes, listening to them going on, Legacy wanted to scream: she knew as well as they did that these weren't the ideal circumstances for training.

And the closest she was going to get to weight lifting this morning was stirring this pot of porridge.

Alone in the kitchen without either one of her friends, aware that Gia and Villy Sal and all her other competitors were currently training at the top facility in the world, Legacy found herself stirring harder and harder.

She gritted her teeth and stirred and tried not to think about defending her title or whether the editorials in the *Nova Times* were right when they suggested that her victory had been a fluke. She tried not to think about that, except that, of course, it was *all* she could think about, and so she stirred harder and harder until suddenly, with a snap, the tension in the porridge gave.

Legacy lifted the spoon out of the cauldron. It had broken right at its neck. The useful end had sunk down to the bottom of the thickening porridge.

"Flirp," she muttered, copying the swear word she used to hear older kids at the academy use when they whiffed an easy overhead. Then, almost immediately, she heard someone behind her and blushed.

"Leggy?"

It was Hugo's timid voice. Legacy turned to see him hovering in the doorway. Since Legacy had left to go to the city, he and Ink together had taken on some of her tasks, looking after the smaller and

3

less capable littles. Ink had taken responsibility for entertaining them. Hugo seemed to have taken responsibility for keeping them fed. He knew his way around the kitchen like an experienced chef.

His new responsibilities had changed him. He was more dependable, but also more fearful. Now she wished he'd just step forward and say whatever it was he wanted to say.

"What is it, Hugo?" she said. Her voice was sharper than she'd intended.

"Um—there's someone at the front gate."

Legacy doused the cooking fire and put a lid over the cauldron. "Make some sandwiches for lunch, please," she said. "And make one for Zaza *without* jam."

It was a precaution developed from experience: Zaza plus jam meant sticky handprints on every surface she could reach.

She left Hugo in the kitchen to go investigate the visitor. It was a rare event, and she was wary of who might be asking for entry. In the past, before she went to the city, she might have been excited about the novelty of a stranger. She could remember the old days, when her father would welcome travelers in for the night. He'd put them to work—repairing light fixtures, painting cracked walls—to earn their room and board. Over dinner, shared with these strangers, it had been fun to hear new stories from new parts of the provinces.

But now times had changed, as Legacy was well aware. She'd had a hand in changing them. When she won the national tournament, she'd made a spectacularly powerful enemy in High Consul Silla, otherwise known as the Queen since her younger days dominating the tennis court. Silla had smiled as she presented Legacy with the check, but she'd hissed threats under her breath.

4

In that moment, Legacy had felt bold—even reckless. *Come after me*, she had said to Silla. *I dare you.*

Now, wearing her apron, holding the broken end of the spoon, Legacy shivered at the memory. What had inspired such boldness in her heart? Was it knowing that Silla was her mother's sister? Was it winning the nationals, beating Gia, feeling light radiating out of her body and pushing back against Gia's darkness?

Both were hard to imagine. Walking through the great room toward the front door, noticing the mess the littles had left on the long table, she couldn't escape the nagging fear that it was someone else— some other version of herself, maybe—who had won the nationals. The *real* her—the Legacy she'd become once again after fleeing to the orphanage—wasn't a champion. The real her used her speed to round up the littles for bath time, used her strength to stir porridge, and barely radiated enough light to see her own two feet when the sun had fallen on an after-dinner training session on the old court in the forest.

She paused before she reached the front door. Whoever was out there could have been sent by Silla. The thought sent shivers down her spine.

But then Legacy shook her head. If Silla hadn't come to get her yet, she wasn't planning to get her in the forest. Sometimes, at night, struggling to fall asleep in her orphanage cot—so different from the large, brocade-draped bed she'd slept in at the academy—Legacy wondered whether Silla was planning something bigger than a quiet attack in the forest.

A public humiliation, maybe. A loss in front of everyone in the republic.

Something to cause people to give up on Legacy Petrin. To

5

restore their faith in Silla and protect her solid shape on the Tapestry of Granity.

Legacy could still remember those final points in her match against Gia, when she'd looked up at the tapestry and seen the outlines of Silla's form starting to waver, how her face and her form were no longer recognizable. The tapestry was a reflection of the people's will. It showed the form of the leader they believed in. For Silla to remain high consul, for her vote to matter more than the votes of the other senators, her form on the tapestry had to be clear. And it had been, for years. Until that moment when Legacy beat Gia and refused to pledge the victory to the high consul.

Then, Silla's shape on the tapestry had started to blur.

Legacy had seen it.

Everyone in the stands had seen it, too. The announcers had even pointed it out.

It was, of course, only a momentary flicker—a few minutes of real change, a few hours of a strange blurriness around her hair and her shoulders. Then Silla's form on the tapestry had grown clear again, and now—since Legacy had returned to the provinces, and Silla had stepped up her popular provincial outreach programs—it was clearer than ever.

At first, in the days after Legacy and her friends had arrived at the orphanage, every stray sound—every twig snapping underfoot—had caused Legacy to startle. She was sure Silla would send an agent to arrest her or—worse—to harm her in a way that would look like a "tragic accident." But as the days wore on without any confrontations, Legacy had begun to wonder whether there was a more complicated plan afoot, some less obvious way to prevent Legacy from threatening Silla's power again.

At least that's what Legacy told herself as she approached the front door of the orphanage. Still, before opening it, she paused for a moment and gripped the porridge spoon handle. She noticed—with some satisfaction—that its broken end was quite sharp and pointy.

She cracked open the door. "Hello?" she called out.

"I'm here with books!" a voice answered. "Books for sale! Books of all kinds! Cookbooks, game books, storybooks, and history books!"

Legacy opened the door a bit wider. If this was one of Silla's agents, she definitely wasn't paying enough. He was ancient, if you could tell anything from the curving slope of his back. But that also could have been because of the giant sack he'd slung over his shoulder.

Legacy opened the door fully and smiled. "Come in," she said. "I'll see if my father is . . ."

She trailed off. She knew her father would be napping again. Since she'd come back from the city, he'd been having trouble sleeping at night and had taken to falling into deep daytime slumbers.

"Actually," she said, "why don't you show me what you have? My father's always loved an old tome—the dustier and the drier the better."

The peddler heaved the sack to the floor, where it fell with a dusty thud. Then he peered at Legacy. "My goodness," he said. "You look just like Legacy Petrin!"

Legacy smiled modestly. "I am," she said. "I mean, that's me. Legacy Petrin."

The peddler pulled a pair of crooked glasses out of the front pocket of his patched vest. Then he held them over his nose and leaned forward to peer at Legacy's face.

"Astonishing," he said. "A spitting image! Like two berries on a branch."

7

"Y-yes," Legacy stammered. "That's me, Legacy Petrin."

But the peddler didn't seem to be listening. "Legacy Petrin!" he was saying, turning back to his sack of books and beginning to rifle through it. "Now, *there* you have a champion. I just saw her in the city, you know. I was there on my yearly trip, prowling the antique shops for rare books on stringcraft. She was playing some charity match against one of those Sindril twins, the ones from Capari. I can't remember which one—but either way, Legacy crushed him. A *dominant* performance, it really was."

Legacy tried to smile politely, but she found herself getting annoyed. The littles would wake from their nap at any moment, and then they'd be swarming the orphanage, demanding the corn porridge that she hadn't managed to make, and here was this ancient peddler making up stories about her exploits.

Legacy cleared her throat. "Mr., um, Mr. Peddler. I *am* Legacy Pet—"

"It wasn't just her strength or her endurance," the peddler said, interrupting her with a quick shake of his head. "Though, goodness knows those are impressive enough. It was her *light*. Stronger than ever. Much stronger than it was, even, at the nationals. You know what they say, of course: 'No one shines brighter than Legacy Petrin!' Never been a truer thing said in the republic."

Legacy watched him pulling books out of his sack, arranging them on the floor. What was he talking about? What was this match he'd imagined, between the Sindril twins and—well—*her*? How could *her* grana be stronger than Legacy's own?

"Here, let me show you," the peddler was saying, pulling a folded brochure out of one of his books.

8

Legacy opened it. An advertisement, by the looks of it. Something about a charity tennis match, played between someone named Wick Sindril and . . . *National Champion Legacy Petrin.*

Legacy stared. All proceeds, apparently, went to Silla's Fund for the Deserving Children of Minori.

"A *truly* dominant performance," the peddler was saying, still shaking his head in something resembling awe. "You should have heard the crowd! They love her. Oh, how the people of this country love her!"

"How they love *me!*" Legacy shouted before instantly turning bright red in embarrassment.

"Oh?" The peddler straightened up and peered at her. He finally seemed to have heard what she was saying. Now he furrowed his brow, taking in her corn-porridge-splattered apron, the broken spoon she was holding instead of a racket.

He smiled. "Oh, yes, dear, of course! Of *course* they do!"

Legacy narrowed her eyes. Was that pity she heard in his voice? Was he trying to *soothe* her? She was about ready to tell him to scram, when Pippa came rushing down the stairs.

"Books!" she cried, nearly tumbling into the peddler.

"He was just leaving," Legacy said through gritted teeth. "Sorry, Pippa. No books for us today."

But Pippa was already clutching a dusty old tome with a faded green cover. The title, *Stringing for Doubles,* was stamped on the front in what looked like red wax.

"Oh, but I've always wanted to have this!" Pippa was saying. "It's an ancient tradition—doubles matches, two players on each side, hardly even remembered these days! There's no doubt there's something good in here."

Legacy sighed and reached into her pocket, where she always kept a few coins.

The peddler pocketed them, gathered his books back into his sack, stooped under its weight, fumbled around for his spectacles, and finally smiled up at Legacy.

"You must be such a big fan," he said.

Legacy furrowed her brow. "A fan of whose?"

"To even go so far as to style your hair the same way. And wear the same clothing! I hear it's a fad that's sprung up all through the provinces. Young girls just like you, dressing and acting like Legacy Petrin. Of course, city dwellers have done it forever, wearing their hair in Villy Sal pompadours, or Gia braids. But Legacy Petrin—she gave us provincials something to copy!"

"I'm not *copying*," Legacy said, "I'm—"

"No use protesting," the peddler said, shaking his head indulgently. "You've done an excellent job, I must say, nearly identical, though of course she struck me as a good bit taller than you—"

Legacy swallowed her irritation. She gave the peddler what she hoped was a polite smile, then led him out the front door. And only when his stooped form had grown small at the end of the long driveway leading to the orphanage did she take the brochure out of her apron pocket and stare at it again.

That photograph of Legacy Petrin, playing a charity match in the city: It was her! It was absolutely *her*!

She was so caught up in the brochure that she didn't notice Javi approaching until he was looking at the brochure over her shoulder.

"A charity match?" he said. Legacy jumped. "When did you do this? Where was I, in the forest?"

"I *didn't* do it," Legacy said. "That's not me. I mean—it *is* me. But *that* wasn't *me*."

Javi looked at her and then looked at the brochure and then looked at her again.

"I . . . don't understand," he said.

"Hey—this stupid book isn't even about doubles!" Pippa shouted, rushing out the front door. She was waving the book over her head, trying to catch the peddler's attention, but he'd already turned at the end of the driveway. Pippa stopped, deflated. "It's about some kind of 'vivification' thing that sounds a little kooky to me," she muttered, "and it's written horribly, and— What's that?"

Legacy sighed. Pippa, too, was staring at the brochure. Now Javi grabbed it and shook it so that it fell open.

Inside, there were more pictures: Legacy Petrin smiling. Legacy Petrin handing a big novelty check to a group of children. Legacy Petrin wearing a beautiful bright blue tennis dress that seemed to shimmer even in the photograph. Legacy Petrin kissing an infant held out by an adoring mother.

She looked amazing.

"It's—it's *you*," Javi said.

"But it's not!" Legacy said. "I didn't play a charity match in the city. I've been here, making corn porridge and getting littles into pajamas!"

Pippa cocked her head to one side and peered at the dangling brochure. "It looks a lot like you," she said.

"Where did you get this?" Javi said. "From that peddler I saw heading off down the driveway?"

Legacy nodded.

Javi shook his head in irritation. "One of Silla's tricks," he said.

"She probably sent that peddler here with this brochure. Had the photographs mocked up herself. Got some city dweller to dress up as you, gave her something that looked like your racket. Don't worry about it. She's trying to get in your head, distract you from training."

Pippa nodded. "He's right, Leg. This looks to me like one of Silla's dirty tricks."

Legacy glanced at them both. "But the grana," she said, gesturing to a paragraph in the brochure that described how Legacy's light was stronger than ever. "If she's not me, how did she summon *that*?"

"C'mon," Javi said. "You don't think Silla can put on a light show? Get the cameras set up in the right places, then use paper lanterns, torches behind screens, what have you?"

Pippa was nodding. "Classic Silla. Get it out of your mind, Leg."

"Let's get down to the court and hit some balls," Javi said. "The best defense against this is training. Reps and sweat, sweat and reps."

"And meditation," Pippa said, her nostrils flaring in aggravation. "Mindfulness and meditation."

Legacy sighed. This difference in coaching philosophy—hard physical work versus psychological training—was becoming the source of increasing tension between Legacy's friends.

Javi ignored Pippa. "The Capari Open is in two weeks. You can't let yourself get distracted by some sort of ploy with a phony brochure and a book peddler. Capari's essential. If you play badly there, the whole country will think you were just a flash in the pan."

"A fluke," Pippa said.

"Got it," Legacy said.

"A counterfeit," Pippa was saying. Now she was just enjoying showing off the vocabulary she'd learned from poring through old stringing tomes. "A mock-up, a pseudo-concoction, a simulated, spurious—"

"*Got it!*" Legacy said.

Pippa smiled apologetically. Javi started going on about some new ingredient he was thinking of adding to his muscle-bulk smoothie. Then they started bickering again about the best approach to Legacy's training, and while they were distracted, Legacy looked down at the brochure.

This other Legacy, whoever she was: Her dress was so beautiful. *She* was so beautiful. So fierce, swinging her racket with all her might.

She seemed like a champion. Like the kind of champion who could win at Capari.

Now Legacy looked down at her apron, smudged with wild honey, and her chapped hands, gripping the porridge spoon.

But who was *this* Legacy? And what could she do, other than go inside and stir up a fresh batch of corn porridge?

CHAPTER TWO

BACK TO THE BASICS

It was a beautiful summer afternoon in the Forest of Cora. The sun had scattered bright patches on the forest floor, and the gold leaves from the drammus tree waved this way and then that in the wind. It was a perfect temperature for training, and Legacy was blowing it.

In her defense, there was a lot going on. The littles had come out to watch, and for a few minutes they'd sat obediently in the stands until they got distracted by shiny buzzbugs. Then they were yelling and chasing them in every direction.

Gus—his wings unfurled, his hooves pounding the grass, faint curls of smoke emerging from his nostrils—was trying to focus on retrieving Legacy's cross-courts and returning them, with a little extra fire and smoke, hard down the line. But every so often a little ran out on court and threw her arms around his neck or kissed his velvety snout.

This—as Javi liked to remind her—was not how pyruses at the academy were kept in peak training condition. At the academy, of course, they were treated cruelly. They were kept underfed. You weren't meant to pet them. Their anger made them fierce.

Neglected and mean, they kept the academy kids in line with their expertly aimed fireballs, just as the lurals—the illegal leopard-wolves that Silla bred to race students on the academy track—kept them on their toes.

Legacy knew that wasn't the way. At the academy, she'd nursed Gus back to health, and he'd been a better training partner ever since. But here, it was true, things had perhaps gotten a bit out of hand.

Since he'd followed her to the orphanage, Gus slept in the old tool-shed, the closest thing they had to the academy barn. But most nights, at least one of the littles snuck out to sleep next to him.

And by morning, at least three or four other littles had crept out of their beds to eat their breakfast in his stable, so that by the time Legacy came to lead him to the court, his muzzle was often sticky with honey.

With each passing day, Gus had gotten friendlier and happier until now it was hard for him to even summon a basic fireball. Now he lolloped around like a puppy, receiving as much love as he could get, gazing at Legacy over the net as though he'd rather lick her than aim a fireball at her face.

Still, obediently, he was doing his part to participate in the series of drills Javi had designed. They didn't have the silk kites they had at the academy to help her run with a sense of lightness, or the academy whirlpools, or a stable full of lurals to help her run with a sense of urgency. But, Javi said, they had enough to get back to the basics: cross-courts and drives, volleys and lobs.

So Legacy and Gus had returned to the fundamentals. Today it was cross-court/drive. Legacy tried to focus on the shots she was supposed to be hitting. But the more she told herself to focus for Javi, the harder it was. Instead of minding the subtle movements of her shoulder, her elbow, her wrist, she found her thoughts drifting to the fact that it was for her sake that Javi had abandoned his successful career as an academy builder who helped train the athletes. Instead of focusing on her footwork, she remembered that Pippa had left all the luxuries of life in the city in order to follow them to the provinces. Instead of perfecting the transfer of her weight from her back foot to her front foot, she thought about that other Legacy.

Because—if that brochure was real—her light was stronger than Legacy's own.

And because, like everyone else, Legacy knew the saying the peddler had repeated: "No one shines brighter than Legacy Petrin."

Which meant that—if that brochure was real—that other Legacy was *the* Legacy.

Which meant that *she* was something else altogether.

And which also meant that Legacy was having a very hard time focusing on her cross-courts.

She'd missed another easy shot, and now Javi was yelling again about reps and sweat, and Pippa was calling out mantras to keep her mind in the present, and Legacy headed back to the baseline to start all over again.

"She just needs to let her thoughts go," Pippa shouted.

"What she needs is more reps!" Javi yelled back.

Legacy gritted her teeth. What she *needed*, she thought, was to win Capari.

Which was how she'd justify the sacrifices her friends had made, and how she'd prove that her win at the nationals wasn't a fluke, a mock-up, a spurious—

"*Focus!*" Javi roared from the sideline.

Legacy winced.

One of Gus's fireballs had flown so close to her cheek that she felt a singe of heat in her eyebrow.

"Maybe she needs a break!" Pippa called from her place on the referee stand.

Legacy felt herself turning red.

"You're tired, right?" Pippa said.

"Of course she isn't tired!" Javi said. "Reps and sweat, sweat and reps!"

"Leg," Pippa called, "do you need a rest?"

Legacy shook her head. "Let me try again," she said. She looked over the net at Gus. "Try me again!" she called.

Back to the baseline.

She knew she could do this. Backhand cross-courts were her favorite shots. It was a drill like second nature, a drill she'd done over and over since she first started playing, and now, if she focused, she could get back in the groove.

Soon her shots were pinging off her racket again, and her fingers had started to tingle, a sure sign that she'd soon be glowing. She felt the ball striking the sweet spot of her strings, the grass giving way under-foot, her swing moving freely through the fresh forest air.

But as soon as she thought that—the fresh forest air—Legacy found herself thinking that now she was representing the forestry province. That now, in fact, she was representing all the provinces.

That's what she'd promised after her victory against Gia. She'd pledged her victory to the provinces, not to Silla. And in doing that, she'd made a clear statement that she resented the way Silla had been channeling funds away from the provinces and into the city. At the time, making that pledge had seemed like a reasonable thing to do, but now it just felt so . . . huge. Her boldness in standing up to Silla. Her strength in beating Gia, Silla's obvious favorite. The way her light had pushed back against Gia's darkness until Silla's figure on the tapestry started to blur.

It all felt so huge that it was pressing down on her shoulders. The weight of it was grinding her into the ground so that she began to feel smaller and smaller. Or she was growing smaller and smaller. And the court was growing longer. It was true: the court was longer than she'd remembered, and the net was higher, and she had to swing with all her might just to get the ball to clear it—

"Legacy!" Javi was striding out onto the court. "That's the third basic drive you've missed in a row. You're out of control! You're hitting everything long."

Legacy furrowed her brow. Long?

She glanced at Gus, who stood on the baseline with smoke flowering out of his nose. Sure enough, the grass behind him was littered with stray balls.

How had that happened? She was sure the last three drives would go short. The court seemed to stretch endlessly before her, so long she was certain she wouldn't have the power to get the ball over the net, let alone *long*—

"This is getting serious," Javi was saying in his most serious voice. "You only have fourteen days to train before we leave for the Capari Open. You can be sure Gia's been training nonstop, not to mention Villy Sal and everyone else. And if Silla was willing to stoop to string-bind tampering last time, you can only imagine what she'll be willing to resort to this time, now that you made a fool of her at the national championships."

Pippa had hopped down from the referee stand and crossed the court to join them.

"Maybe she needs a rest," Pippa said. "Some time to meditate, to—"

"Maybe she needs to get back to work!" Javi said. "Sweat and reps, reps and sweat—"

"What she needs is to visualize herself succeeding!" Pippa said. "What she needs is to meditate on success!"

Legacy bit her lip. She was letting them down. She was letting everyone down. They'd all given up so much to come with her to the forest: their spots at the academy, which would have led to lucrative professions; their privileges as city dwellers; their safety, if Silla's threats meant anything. They'd given all that up because they believed in her, and in return all she needed to do was to play better than ever before. And here she was hitting all her shots long.

"I could have sworn," she murmured, "that those shots were going short."

Javi pulled a piece of grass and started chewing on it huffily. "They weren't," he said.

Legacy flushed. It had been a long time since Javi had gotten under her skin like this.

Pippa glared at Javi. Then she put one arm around Legacy's shoulders. "Come on," she said. "It's been a long day, and I've got something to show you back in the attic."

CHAPTER THREE

CLOUDS OVER THE FOREST

The first thing Legacy noticed was how dark it was. The window in the eaves had been covered up with rough cloth, through which no natural light could shine. On every available surface, there were candles of all sizes and heights, but they gave off only a wan light, especially the ones that flickered strange-colored flames: red, pale blue, even black. Their shadows flickered up the walls in long tongues.

And then, of course, there were the books. Scattered everywhere and stacked ten-, sometimes twenty-high.

"Come in, come in," Pippa said, leading the way down a tiny twisty pathway cleared through the towers of books. On the other end of the path was a small circular clearing. Pippa sat down on the floor and gestured to Legacy to join her.

"Pip!" Legacy said. "What on earth have you been doing in here?"

"It's to set the mood," Pippa said distractedly. "It's all about mood."

Legacy's laugh sounded more nervous than she'd hoped it would. "Okay, well, my mood is a little creeped out. Can we open the blinds?"

Pippa ignored her. "Sit," she said, gesturing again to the space on the floor. "You're on your feet all day, either chasing after the littles or chasing after Gus's fireballs. You're tired. You're overworked. No wonder you're not playing your best."

Legacy sighed. "Thanks, Pip," she said. "But it's not even that I'm all that tired. I don't know what happened out there. I could have sworn my shots were going short. I didn't even think they'd clear over the net."

Pippa was leaning forward, listening very closely. "You thought those shots wouldn't clear over the net?" she said.

Legacy nodded. "I was thinking about how I beat Gia, and how I pledged my victory to the provinces instead of to Silla, and how her form started to blur on the tapestry, and how she threatened me right there on center court and said she'd come after me."

Pippa's forehead was furrowed in concentration. "You were thinking about all that, and it seemed as though your shots wouldn't clear over the net?"

"I just started to feel—I don't know, *heavy*. Like something was pressing down on me. Like I was getting smaller, and the net was starting to grow, and it seemed as though nothing I could ever hit would ever clear over that growing net."

Now Pippa started tapping her temple. "Sounds to me like you're letting the noise in. You're dwelling on the past. You're imagining the future. When you're out there, you're not in the moment."

Legacy frowned. This speech was starting to sound like something Javi would call "mental mumbo jumbo." She had only two weeks until Capari, when she'd need to defend her recent victory, and she didn't have time to think about the past, the future, *or* the present moment: she just needed to start playing better.

"I know it seems abstract," Pippa said, placing a thick candle between them. "But please hear me out. Focus on the flame."

Legacy looked at the flame. It was leaping around, doing a little dance.

"Now close your eyes," Pippa said, "and take a breath."

Legacy took a breath. Then she took another one.

She was starting to get antsy.

How long was Pippa going to keep her here in the attic? Her breaths started to come faster.

"No," Pippa said. "I mean take a *real* breath. An inhalation so big it fills your whole belly like a balloon. And an exhalation so big you feel your belly button get drawn to your spine."

Legacy breathed. And this time, she really breathed. As she breathed in, she felt something kind flow into her body. She felt it enter her veins. She felt it spread to her fingertips and her toes.

And as the air rushed out her nose, she felt as though a weight had been taken off her shoulders.

Then she breathed again. She listened to the sound of it. Her breath—in and out—sounded like wind sighing through the leaves of the forest. She felt herself melting into the sound of her breath. She was the wind and the trees at once. She felt herself taking root in the attic.

"Yes," Pippa said. "Yes. Just focus on your breath. And if you get distracted by a thought, let the thought go. Just watch it, I mean. Don't think it. Watch it like a cloud in the sky. Just let that cloud float peacefully by."

And so Legacy breathed. She let herself sway in the wind of her own breath. And if she remembered how much Javi and Pippa had given up, she made that thought a cloud in the sky over the forest. She watched it. And she let it float by.

And if she remembered that other Legacy in the brochure, she made it a cloud, too, and she let it float by.

And soon all her thoughts were floating by, over the whispering canopy of the forest.

"Now," Pippa said, "I want you to picture a time when you were happy."

It took a moment for such a time to come to her. First, her mind was blank. Then, on the blank floor of her mind, she saw the little flame dancing. It reminded her of the time she and her father and her best friend, Van, had gone to the summer carnival. There were torches everywhere. Everyone had been in costume: her and Van and the littles and even her father. She and Van together had dressed as a dingbat. She'd been a bell, he'd been a bat: a dingbat. It had been her father's idea. He wasn't so stern back then, and he wasn't so tired, and he'd always had a weakness for the summer carnival. He liked to imagine interesting costumes, often based on corny wordplay. He liked to climb to the attic, find rolls of old fabric and cardboard and paint, and drag them all out and create something new. To give them all new identities for the day. To help them all become brand-new people, so that Van wasn't an orphan, Legacy hadn't lost her mother, and he hadn't lost his wife.

So Legacy had wrapped herself in an enormous structure of silver cardboard shaped like a bell, and Van had worn a stretchy black costume with wings. They'd run from booth to booth, holding hands, and without Van even saying it, Legacy knew he wanted a stick of spun honey, and without her even saying it, he knew that she wanted to play the game where you threw feathered darts at a target.

That's how close they were, she and Van. It was as though they had a secret, silent language, one they'd spoken for as long as Legacy could remember. And they were the only two people in the world who knew how to speak it. Van knew dreams she'd never dared to admit out loud.

It was he who knew she wanted to go train at the academy, back when she was still refusing to say it.

That night, at the carnival, when they ran from booth to booth and the sun set and the stars rose, Van was the only one in the world who knew that every time Legacy saw a star, she wished that she could become the greatest tennis player in the whole republic.

They'd run together, hand in hand, and they'd found her father again. He'd stayed with the littles, dressed as robbers and fairies, mermaids and lurals—and her father had worn a purple wig. Hidden away in their costumes, their true identities known only to one another, they'd all felt so perfectly free that they ended up dancing. Even Van, with his limp. Even her father, who generally felt there were too many important tasks to get done to leave time for dancing.

Remembering that—her father, grinning, swinging his arms in his awkward way while Van twisted beside him—Legacy felt tears begin to come to her eyes.

She wasn't breathing anymore. She'd opened her eyes, and the tears were rolling down her cheeks. The flame had blurred. It no longer looked like a dancer.

"Oh, Leg," Pippa said. She blew out the candle and leaned forward to hug her. "What's wrong? What is it that's bugging you?"

"I was just thinking of a time when I went to the summer carnival with my father and Van," Legacy said. "It seems like forever ago. I haven't heard from Van since he left. He hasn't responded to one of my letters. And my father—he just hasn't been the same since I came back from the academy. He's tired all the time. He can't keep up with orphanage business."

Pippa nodded. "Did he always have that cough?"

24

Legacy shook her head. "Not like that," she said. "That happened while I was away. And I can't help thinking—"

Pippa furrowed her brow. "What?"

"I can't help thinking it's my fault. That he was so worried about me when I was away, and—"

"No," Pippa said. "It's not your fault. You were pursuing your own destiny."

"Sure," Legacy said, "but thanks to me pursuing my destiny, my father's sick, Van doesn't answer my letters, and Javi gave up his position at the academy. And I know that if I could win Capari, and show the country that he's the best builder in or out of the academy, and prove that it doesn't take Silla's support to be champion, it would all be worthwhile. But when I think of that, I feel scared. Because what if I can't? The weight of it—it just feels so heavy . . ."

Pippa was nodding. "It all feels so heavy that you start to feel small, and the net starts to feel big, and that's why your shots are going way long."

Legacy smiled through her tears. "You understand," she said.

"Of course I do," Pippa said. "You think I never felt any pressure, back at the academy? When I was the daughter of the country's best stringer?"

"So how did you deal with it?" Legacy said.

Pippa shook her head. "I don't know," she said. "Javi would say it's all about getting back out on court."

"Sweat and reps," Legacy said, imitating Javi's sternest builder voice.

"Reps and sweat," Pippa said, puffing out her chest and holding her skinny arms out so they'd look buff.

Legacy started laughing. It felt good. It was the first time she'd laughed—really laughed—in a few days.

"Thanks for listening, Pip," she said.

Pippa was still puffing her chest out and speaking in an exaggeratedly low Javi voice. "Now, if we could just find some mothwing powder for muscle bulk—"

"*Guys!*"

It was the real Javi, bursting into the attic, upsetting several towers of books and waving a copy of the *Nova Times* over his head.

"Did you see this?" he said, dropping the paper in Legacy's lap.

The front page showed a big image of Gia—her braid whipping around and her muscles taut as her racket struck the ball—under the headline DARKER DAYS—INSIDE THE NEWEST DEVELOPMENTS OF THE ACADEMY'S TOP PLAYER.

Legacy's throat tightened as she read the story. Behind her, Javi offered commentary. "They're saying her grana's darker than dark now," he said. "Darker than the nighttime. So dark, her opponents start to see shapes. So dark even people in the crowd start to have nightmares—"

Now Legacy's stomach was tightening as well. It had been hard enough, facing Gia's darkness back when she was playing her at the national championships. And now it was darker than ever, and Legacy's own grana had wavered. Her grana was strongest when she was playing confidently and well—but recently she couldn't even keep her drives in, let alone summon the kind of light she'd need to compete against a darkness like the one the *Nova Times* was describing.

Which was why it was so unsettling when she turned the page to find a two-page spread behind the opening picture of Gia, featuring the exploits of Legacy Petrin.

Legacy Petrin!

There she was: that other Legacy. False Legacy.

In the pictures, she was on court, hitting what seemed to be a blistering overhead slam; and she was off court, signing autographs for a bunch of admiring children; and she was dressed in a gown, standing under an enormous chandelier, laughing with a kid who stood in the shadows and looked strangely like Van.

Legacy's hands trembled while she held the paper. The words began to blur as she read about Legacy attending a charity gala in support of Silla's initiatives in the provinces; about Legacy playing an exhibition match and revealing stronger-than-ever light grana; about Legacy beating a star player from Capari by causing a blinding column of light to move over the court.

At the bottom of the page, there was an article about how many children in the provinces had begun dressing up like Legacy: wearing their hair in her loose style, paired with her signature burlap dress. There was a picture of False Legacy playing a match in front of a crowd of other Legacys.

Legacy turned the spread to Pippa and Javi. "You guys really think this is just a ruse to distract me from my training?"

Pippa bit her lip. "She really does look a lot like you. And if this is a ruse, there are a whole lot of people who are in on it."

Javi peered closer. "I mean, I guess the good news is that people seem to love Legacy Petrin?"

Legacy stared at the photographs of this girl with her name, who looked exactly like her. Like her, but taller. And with stronger grana. And, by the looks of it, a whole lot more popular in the city.

Looking at herself—but not herself—in the paper, Legacy couldn't help but remember that moment in Pippa's father's workshop at the academy, when she and Javi and Pippa had seen themselves in the tapestry.

But this wasn't a tapestry. This was real life. And another version of her was in the city.

Javi was still peering over her shoulder. "I mean, people really love this girl. It says here that they've been flocking in record numbers to the charity matches she's playing in support of Silla's initiatives in the provinces."

"And that she's accepted Silla's sponsorship," Pippa said.

"And that her public appearances have been boosting Silla's popularity," Javi said.

Pippa whistled. "Look at those numbers! Since 'Legacy Petrin' signed on, support for Silla's provincial outreaches has gone through the roof."

Javi nodded. "It just goes to show how influential players can be. I mean—"

Legacy tugged the paper away. "Guys!" she said. "You're talking about her as though she's a real player!"

Pippa and Javi exchanged a quick glance. Legacy wondered whether they were hiding something, or whether they just thought she was overreacting.

"She's not real! *I'm* real. *I'm* the real Legacy Petrin."

"Of course," Javi said.

Pippa patted Legacy's arm. "I'm sure she's just some talentless look-alike Silla dragged in from the provinces."

"But she's not just a look-alike," Legacy said. "I mean, she looks more like me than *I* do. And look at this stuff about her light grana. They're saying she can summon columns of light, whole waves of light! That's more than I did at the national championships!"

Javi chuckled. "She doesn't just look more like you than you do," he said. "She might also *play* more like you than you do."

Pippa gave Javi a shove that was less subtle than she'd probably hoped. Then she smiled brightly at Legacy. "Let me do some research," she said. "Maybe it's possible that some sort of foul play is going on."

Legacy frowned. "'Maybe it's possible'? This is Silla we're talking about!"

Pippa sighed. "Okay, you're right. It's probably more than possible. But how is it helping you to focus on this other Legacy?"

"It's only distracting you more," Javi said.

"And really, you already have enough on your mind," Pippa said.

"Certainly enough," Javi said, somewhat less tactfully, "to prevent you from optimum training."

Legacy felt her stomach sink. *Oh. Right.*

Training.

Another day of training. An early-morning run, followed by breakfast, followed by agility drills in the forest, then lunch, followed by afternoon practice, followed by after-dinner practice.

Another day of muscle-bulk smoothies. Another day of the net growing and the court lengthening and her shots flying long, and her light grana showing up weaker than that other Legacy's.

Across from her, Pippa was giving her a sympathetic glance. "Maybe," Pippa said, "we should take a little break."

"It's always breaks with you!" Javi said. "Rest and breaks and mental—"

Legacy glanced at one of Pippa's candles. The bright little flame was dancing again.

"She's right, Javi," Legacy said. "I need a break. We all need a break. And I have an idea. Have you guys ever been to a summer carnival?"

CHAPTER FOUR

THE HOUSE OF MAGICAL MIRRORS

The next morning, Legacy stopped by her father's room as soon as the sun rose. He spent more time in his room now, poring over orphanage paperwork on the desk he used to keep so organized. Now it was piled high with stacks of paper, water glasses, mugs, pens and pencils, half-eaten honey cakes. When Legacy entered, he looked up at her with a frown.

"Papa," she started, trying not to think about how much his desk had changed. "I—"

A fit of coughing interrupted her.

Waiting for him to finish, she tried to imagine him as he'd been that other summer, when he'd taken her and Van to the carnival. How excited he'd been about the costumes he'd imagined; how he'd glowed with pride whenever anyone gave them compliments. She blinked back the tears that had blurred her vision.

"Papa, when are you going to see the doctor about that cough? I'll pay. We've got the money from—"

He glared at her. When she'd returned from the city and handed him the envelope, he'd taken only enough money to cover a year's worth of food for the littles, as well as a few orphanage repairs. The rest he'd given back. And since then, any mention of the money she'd made by disobeying him and going into the city—winning the national championships and attracting the wrath of the high consul—still darkened his mood, though he'd forgiven her for her decision to go.

"Not now, Legacy. I have work to do here. Bills to pay. Children's futures to organize."

Legacy swallowed. She thought for a moment, then started again. "I was just remembering the summer carnival," she said. "The one when you dressed me and Van as a dingbat?"

For a moment, her father looked up and smiled the old smile: so that his eyes crinkled and his whole face seemed to shine. Almost as soon as it had come, however, the smile faded, and he focused again on the check he was writing.

"I thought maybe I'd take Pippa and Javi," Legacy tried again.

Her father didn't look up. "Sure," he said. "Take the day off. Hugo can help me out here. He helped out while you were away."

Legacy winced. She didn't like to think about how Hugo and Ink had been forced to step up and act more adult while she was off playing tennis. Now Hugo had changed, and Ink was quieter, too. She had less of the babyish exuberance she'd had when Legacy left. But even so: Legacy needed this. She needed a day to feel like a kid herself, to feel less of that heaviness on her shoulders, to try to get her old lightness back so she could play like her old self.

She looked at her father and made one last attempt. "Papa, you want to come with us? We could make up costumes, and—"

Her father's glare cut her off. But maybe he saw her disappointment, because in a moment his face softened a little. "Sweetheart," he said. "Not today. There's too much work to be done here. My records are all out of order and—"

His coughing interrupted him once more. Legacy paused in the doorway. She watched his shoulders heave. He was thinner now. His frame almost looked like a boy's.

She thought of going over to him to hug him. But she didn't want to embarrass him, or make him feel weak, so she hovered there in the doorway until he'd caught his breath.

"Go," he finally said. "Go! Before I change my mind and remember why I can't spare you."

———

When Legacy got to the well, Javi was pulling up a big bucket of water, and Pippa appeared to be carrying a huge pile of laundry.

"What's up?" Legacy asked. "Aren't we going to the carnival?"

"Of course!" Pippa said. Legacy realized that she had painted her face. It looked like she had whiskers.

Pippa blushed. "You're probably noticing the dazzling makeup."

"She's a cat," Javi said.

"A *dazzling* cat," Pippa said, then twirled. Legacy laughed in spite of herself. It had been a long time—maybe since they'd discovered that Pippa's father had been helping Silla tamper with her students' string-binds—since she'd seen Pippa so happy. There was something about costumes, she thought, that brought out the lightheartedness in some people.

Pippa dumped her pile of clothes on the ground. "I found you guys some excellent options," she said, spreading her findings out over the grass and opening her set of paints. Legacy chose an old blue shirt that must have been her father's at some point. Then she found a battered red beret and used a little white paint on her face so that she looked like one of the decorative weavers in the city, the ones who set up looms on street corners and would weave a quick likeness of any tourist and sell it to them for an outrageous price.

Out of the laundry pile, Pippa chose a fuzzy orange bathrobe—"A dazzling *marmalade* cat," she murmured as she cinched it around her waist—and a pair of orange slippers.

And Javi—well, by the time Pippa and Legacy were dressed, Javi was still wearing his typical builder outfit: a black warm-up suit and the sturdy leather sandals that he wore in all weather.

"You have to wear a costume!" Pippa protested.

"I am," Javi said in his surliest voice. "I'm dressed as a builder."

"But you *are* a builder," Pippa said.

"I *was* a builder," Javi said. "Before we came out here, and I had to make do with rocks for weights and a domesticated puppy-pyrus instead of—"

Legacy breathed in so her belly filled like a balloon. She breathed out so her belly button drew in toward her spine. "We're forgetting all that for one day, okay, Javi?"

It took her only a few moments to find one of Hugo's stained aprons in the laundry basket, and once Pippa had fashioned something resembling a chef's hat out of a pillowcase, and Legacy had gone to retrieve a porridge spoon from the kitchen, Javi was a chef.

Legacy took a step back. A cat, a chef, and a weaver. She smiled. The costumes weren't as creative as her father's had been that other summer, but they were enough. For a day, the three of them would escape. For a day, she wouldn't be true Legacy or False Legacy or Legacy at all: she was just a kid from the provinces, dressed up as a weaver, heading out to the carnival with a vain cat and a somewhat disgruntled, truculent chef.

It was a two-hour walk to the carnival on the main roads, one if you knew the shortcuts through the forest. Dressed in their costumes, Legacy and Pippa and Javi made their way under the mixed canopies of the cycapress trees, the moak trees, and the cherish trees. There was soft moss underfoot and whipwings singing in every branch, and for a moment Legacy remembered how frightening she used to find the forest. Back before she'd gone to the city, she'd run through the burned forest and seen the faces of unhappy people in all the charred trunks of the trees. Their dead branches had raked her face like the fingers of witches.

Now, however, the forest didn't seem so threatening. Her father's warnings still rang in her ears—the dangers of a forest after a fire: how easily branches could fall, how quickly a mudslide could start once the root systems had died—but it was clear now that the forest was coming back to life. There was more green; the branches were covered with velvety buds. Everything was alive with smells and sounds, especially when they cleared a small ridge and saw, stretching below them, the tents of the summer carnival.

It was unmistakable: big yellow and green tents clustered around a patch of yellowed and trampled grass. Legacy grinned. As they climbed down the ridge, she could smell the familiar scents of spun sugar, roasted cycapress root, and caramelized kweefruit. Gentle music from the rides filtered up through the smoky air, and even in the daytime the paper lanterns—red, blue, and orange—glowed against the fainter colors of the forest.

As they moved toward the tent where people were dancing, Legacy heard a voice calling. "Sick of stirring corn porridge?" he said. "Come see the world! Don't stay stuck in the forest forever!"

Legacy started. It was as if he'd been with her in the kitchen yesterday morning, reading her thoughts while she stirred the corn porridge. But when she turned, she saw a stranger: a nondescript man behind a little desk with a banner over the top. "SEE THE WORLD!" it read in bright colors.

Legacy approached the man, followed by Javi and Pippa. He was skinny, with sharp elbows and wide eyes and a definite resemblance to a cartoon grasshopper. "Are you two ladies interested in a new career?" he said. "Are you interested in exploring the exotic province known as Minori?"

Pippa and Legacy accepted the pamphlets he was offering: a red sunset over what appeared to be jagged black mountains. The man behind the desk was simultaneously talking and grinning. "The great High Consul Silla has decided to deepen the metium mines of Minori, and that means—jobs! Jobs for all! If you sign up today, we'll even give you an immediate bonus!"

"What kind of jobs?" Legacy said.

The man grinned even wider. "Great jobs, better jobs!"

Javi frowned. "In Minori?" he said. "Somehow I doubt it."

The grin faded from the man's face. A vein twitched under his eye. "Jobs that are part of Silla's new mining initiative! Safer jobs than before, jobs with special benefits!"

Legacy was getting ready to ask a follow-up question when she was shouldered aside by a group of older boys who were eagerly signing paperwork.

"I don't like it," Legacy said, watching as the agent handed them tickets, that excessively enormous grin back in place.

Pippa nodded. "I don't trust it," she said. "I wouldn't trust any improvement project sponsored by Silla."

Javi shrugged. He was carrying a stick with a giant tuft of spun honey. "You shouldn't," he said, his voice muffled slightly by a mouthful of fluffy spun honey. "They've been talking about expanding the metium mines ever since my family moved to Minori. They never have, because if you go any deeper, you'll start hitting the most concentrated mineral deposits. It's dangerous. Like, really, really, really dangerous."

"Maybe they've come up with new techniques," Legacy said. "Maybe—"

"Dancing!" Pippa squealed. Under the blue tent in front of them, a traditional provincial band—hand drums, cherish flutes, a lampognia bagpipe, and a singer with her hair loose, wearing a burlap sack that allowed her to dance freely—was playing one of Legacy's favorite old tunes. A mirrorball cast flecks of lights over the darkened space, and costumed people were dancing. Legacy smiled, and followed her friend, and only stopped when she realized—with a strange shiver down her spine—that about half the people dancing under the tent looked uncannily like her.

Not her in the blue shirt and red beret. Her when she was playing tennis. Her, specifically, when she was beating Gia.

They wore burlap dresses in the style of the dress she'd worn in the finals, and their hair was curly and loose down their backs. They were all carrying rackets and dancing up a storm in their tennis sneakers.

Legacy stared. It was undeniably creepy. How could she walk into the tent and join a bunch of people who'd dressed up to resemble her? Among them, she'd be just another version of herself. Just another Legacy.

She couldn't make herself go in.

Beside her, Pippa pulled up short as well.

"Weird," Javi said.

"They all look like that other Legacy," Pippa said.

Legacy frowned. "They look like *me*," she said, and Pippa smiled apologetically.

"Come on," Pippa said. "I don't feel like dancing."

The three of them lined up outside the House of Magical Mirrors. Javi was still talking, in between giant bites of his candy. "People will die down there," he said. "And even if they don't die, the gases from those deep mineral deposits are going to get piped up and roll around the whole province. What little plant life is still living there will be kaput. Not to mention marine life, and—"

Behind them in line, a tall older woman leaned forward. "That's where you're wrong, sonny," she said. She was wearing purple braids pulled into a topknot, in the style of the tennis announcer Paula Verini. "Jobs are jobs. If you don't want one? Don't take it."

To her side, a man with greased hair and an enormous cardboard flask—the signature accessory of Angelo, Paula's sidekick announcer—nodded in agreement. "Silla's just providing an opportunity for those poor Minorians who otherwise wouldn't be able to eat."

Fake Paula nodded. "A little danger might do them some good, anyway," she said, tossing one of the agent's pamphlets onto the ground and flipping a loose purple braid over her shoulder. "Keep them from getting lazy during those long gray days."

Legacy could see that Javi was starting to bristle. She placed a restraining hand on his shoulder.

Fake Angelo sniffed. "Besides, Legacy Petrin has already traveled there and done a grand opening in the new metium mines. If they're good enough for her, well—"

Fake Paula took him by the elbow, and they shouldered their way past the kids into the House of Magical Mirrors.

"Unbelievable," Legacy said. She glanced back over at Silla's agent. A bigger crowd had gathered around his desk, and he was handing out paperwork left and right. "Javi, based on what you remember—how big are those new mines going to get? How many people do you think could work down there?"

Javi picked up the pamphlet Fake Paula had dropped. He unfolded it for Pippa and Legacy to see. There was a map: a semicircle of mountains, with a silver area denoting the old mine and a red area denoting the new one. The red area stretched five or six times lower than the silver one.

"The old mine," Javi said, "employed just about every person of working age in Minori. This new mine? Even if you employed kids, you couldn't work it just with citizens from Minori. They'll need to bring in workers from all the other provinces."

The doors of the House of Magical Mirrors opened again, and Legacy followed Pippa and Javi inside. Beside them down the long, mirrored corridor, there were dozens of other Legacys. Dozens of other Pippas, dozens of other Javis.

Legacy swallowed. She tried not to think about what Javi had just said: that they'd need provis from all over to fill the new metium mines. She tried not to think of all those provis lining up to get pamphlets, desperate for any kind of work they could find.

She tried not to think about the littles growing up, turning fifteen, the age of adulthood in the provinces. Moving out of the orphanage, looking for work, and possibly heading off to these new mines in Minori.

She tried not to think about Hugo. She tried not to think about Ink and Zaza. She tried not to think about all the littles, in all the provinces, the vast majority of which she couldn't help.

Her winnings from the nationals were enough to keep the orphanage open, but they weren't enough to provide for all the littles once they moved out. That meant that kids like Hugo or Ink or Zaza might end up like those other kids lining up to sign their lives away with Silla's agent.

By the time they reached the next chamber of mirrors, Legacy was sweating. She took off her beret and rubbed one sleeve of her blue shirt across her face, smearing her face paint. Then she looked up to see an image of herself with a tiny, mouse-size body and an enormous face. It was covered in smeared paint, leering back at her evilly.

"Pip," she panted, reaching for Pippa. But her hand only knocked against the cool surface of a mirror.

"Javi!" she said. She reached for him, but once again, her hand struck a cold mirror.

"Guys?" she said, desperately looking around. None of them seemed to be real. Her terror growing, she rushed to the next chamber. There, the reflection of her body was enormous, stretching over the ceiling and down the other side of the room. Suddenly dozens of Pippas and Javis joined her.

"Legacy!" they called.

Legacy, Legacy, Legacy, dozens of false echoes answered.

Legacy spun around. She darted forward. And as she moved, it almost looked as though all the other Legacys were playing tennis: spinning and darting and lunging just as she'd done on the court at the nationals. But the Legacys in the mirror were taller than her, more graceful than her. They moved with a lightness and speed that she lacked.

Legacy was sweating harder. She was clumsier than them, slower. She'd never be able to beat them in a tournament. Not the way she'd been playing in the forest: all her shots flying long, the points so quick she didn't have any time to settle into a rhythm and find her grana. Playing like that, she'd never win a tournament again.

Everywhere she looked, there were other Legacys, Legacys as unrelated to her as that Legacy in the city, the one who was going around in support of Silla's initiatives in the mines. The one who smiled so beautifully in the pictures, and told everyone it was okay for people from the provinces to work in life-threatening conditions. To release gases from the mines that would devastate the whole region.

Legacy's breath was coming faster and faster, tearing jagged rips in her throat. Where were the real Pippa and Javi? Who could she count on in here to help her?

"I can't!" Legacy called out to Pippa and Javi.

Can't, can't, can't! the echoes answered.

"What?" someone answered. *What, what, what!*

"I'm leaving!" she called.

Leaving, leaving, leaving! the echoes taunted while Legacy rushed out of the House of Magical Mirrors, crouched down to catch her breath, and waited for the real Pippa and the real Javi to join her.

"You okay?" Pippa said, tucking Legacy's hair behind her ears.

"That really got you, didn't it?" Javi said. Even he seemed concerned.

41

Legacy looked up at them. "What if I can't win again?" she said. "What if nationals was a fluke, and I can't defend my title?"

"Well," Javi started, "in that case, we're screwed, and—"

Pippa cut him off with one hard shove to the shoulder. "You can," she said. "And you will. And we're here to help you."

Legacy felt the tears starting to prick her eyes. She put her face in her hands. Today—this was supposed to be a day of rest and recuperation. This was how she was going to get her focus back. And now she'd be heading back to practice even more frayed than she'd been when they'd left.

"This was a stupid idea," Legacy said. "Stupid, stupid—"

"Hush," Pippa said, kneeling next to Legacy.

Javi was pacing back and forth in front of them.

"What you're dealing with here," Javi said, "is a loss of confidence. And in that case, the best thing is to get back to the basics. It's all about process: devoting yourself to the movements, the repetitions, the physical routines. I've been working on a new set of drills that will be just the thing. They'll get you out of your head in no time. Just like I've always said, reps and sweat, sweat and reps—"

Pippa narrowed her eyes. "And rest," she said. "And getting in a good headspace."

"And reps," Javi said, looking more determined. "Reps of my new drills in the forest."

CHAPTER FIVE

OPERATION GHOST

Early the next morning, Legacy woke with a headache. Javi was standing next to her bed. He loomed over her like an apparition in the House of Magical Mirrors, a memory that caused Legacy to flinch.

Beside him, Hugo was holding her Tempest and, for some inexplicable reason, a long wooden spoon. And looking very proud to be involved in Legacy's training.

"I'm calling these new drills Operation Ghost," Javi said while they moved down the narrow path that they'd cleared through the cycapress trees. Legacy's legs felt leaden. Yesterday's "rest and recuperation" had sapped what was left of her strength. "Actually," Javi said, "they're pretty basic. It's just a sequence based on run-of-the-mill ghosting, but they're designed to get you to stop thinking so much. You can't be out there on court, remembering your win at nationals, worrying it was a fluke. Wondering whether you can do it again. You've got to be absorbed in the process. You're a pair of feet, a pair of shoulders. You're two hands holding a racket. You're motion and balance, spring and step. You've got to be able to play with your eyes closed."

He went on and on. Legacy had ghosted before—it was a common conditioning drill at the academy, moving around the court while a coach called shots, imagining a ball, swinging as though the imaginary ball really existed. The idea was to focus entirely on your footwork. The idea was to empty the world of anything but the movement of your body, lunging and recovering and running until your thighs burned and your ankles ached.

When Legacy thought about all the problems she'd had in their last training session—the net growing, her shots flying long—she wasn't sure such a basic sequence would work to help. But after her experience in the House of Magical Mirrors, she was willing to try. She glanced behind them to make sure Gus was following, then smiled when he gave her neck a wet, sandpapery kiss.

When they came to the court, Javi and Hugo ducked behind the referee stand, then began rolling something large and black onto the court. A medicine ball, Legacy thought. But it was bigger than that. Then she looked again: it was the corn porridge cauldron she used in the kitchen.

What were they doing?

"First things first," Javi said. "A little warm-up before we start the drills. I call it stirring. No more fancy contraptions like we used to use at the academy. We don't have that luxury. But maybe that's not a bad thing. I'm starting to think the way you train should reflect the life that you live. The *person* you are, not just the player you are. I realized that yesterday, when you were freaking out in the House of Mirrors. I realized—well, I've got to remind you who you are. And to do that, I've got to remember who I am: a builder from the provinces. We've got to use the tools at our fingertips."

Now he pulled a long reed from his pocket. Chewing on a reed was a habit he'd taken up since moving out of the city. Now he broke the reed in half and gave one half to Hugo. Hugo startled, then smiled shyly. They both stuck their reeds in their mouths.

Javi stepped back and gestured at the cauldron. "So here's what you're going to do. Hugo?"

Hugo handed him the porridge spoon. Then Hugo ran to the sideline, filled a bucket with soil, and scampered back over to fill the cauldron with soil as Javi began to stir it around.

"Javi," Legacy said. "We only have twelve days until we leave for Capari. Are you sure I should be spending my training time watching you . . . stirring?"

"You got it," Javi said, and kept stirring.

"But it looks . . . easy."

"It *is* easy," Javi said. "For now. Come here, take over. Imagine the spoon is your racket."

Stirring the dirt with her "Tempest," Legacy's hands found their familiar routine. Then Hugo came back and poured another bucketful of soil in.

"Keep stirring," Javi said. "Keep stirring."

Legacy stirred. She stirred and she stirred, letting her body settle into the familiar process. Soon, her mind began to wander, as though it were a kite on the end of a string. The string kept getting let out more and more. Her mind took the wind and rose up in the air, detached, and detaching ever more.

And then, abruptly, she came back to earth.

Oof. Hugo's last bucket had really made a difference. The cauldron was almost a third of the way full now, and this soil was denser than corn porridge. Her forearms and shoulders were starting to burn.

This wasn't quite as meditative as it had been at the beginning. This was *hard*. And it kept coming. Hugo didn't seem to be tiring at all.

"Keep going," Javi said. "You can't let yourself detach. You have to stay here. You have to stay in the present. That's what the struggle helps with. It keeps your mind in the present moment."

Legacy kept stirring the soil around. She felt her shoulders burn. She felt her forearms starting to tire. She felt herself zoning out again, lulled by the repetitive motion. Then she felt herself pulled back by the new weight of the soil.

As she stirred, she focused on her arms, on the tension and strength in her muscles. She focused on the pattern of her own breath. Hugo gleefully poured more and more soil into the cauldron, but now Legacy didn't feel the extra strain of stirring a heavier load. It was the same burn in her shoulders. It was the same movement of her breath in her chest.

"Okay, that's it!" Javi said. "That's the focus you need to bring to your training!"

Legacy grinned.

It *had* felt good: existing fully inside her body.

Javi sauntered over. "Pippa thinks you'll get your mind in order by sitting around and meditating. But it's about *process*. It's about getting absorbed in each physical step of your game so your mind doesn't have any space to sit down and unfold all the old nightmares. When you're playing tennis, you're a body, not a mind. Your body knows what to do. Your feet know what to do. Got it? Good."

Legacy nodded. "So let's start playing tennis!"

Javi shook his head. "Not yet," he said. "Now's when we start the first step of Operation Ghost."

"Right!" Legacy said. She stepped onto the baseline and smiled. It was good to be out on court. Even though she hadn't been playing well, she'd never stopped loving the feeling of walking out to the T, with the soft grass underfoot.

Now she started ghosting: counting her steps, lunging at the right point, swinging at an imaginary ball hit by an imaginary opponent. She got into a rhythm. She felt her footsteps roll from heel to toe. She felt the shadows of the drammus leaves play over her face. She felt her fingers warm on the grip of her racket.

Javi called shots—"Forehand drop shot! . . . Backhand lob!"—and she retrieved them, or the idea of them, ghosting over and over again until her shoulders were sore. They hurt, but she didn't care. This was what she loved. Moving over the court like this, she didn't have to think about Silla. She didn't have to think about Gia. Her legs burned; her shoulders ached. But as long as her head wasn't getting in the way, she could push through that. She could love pushing through that. She loved the strength in her legs, the freedom in her arms. The way, if she set her feet firmly, she could swing through with all her strength without toppling over.

This was what she was made for, what her body had been created to do. All her mind had to do was get out of the way and let her body respond as it knew how to.

"Excellent!" Javi yelled. His big lopsided grin had returned to his face. Now he was striding out on court, holding something red, a flag, or a bandanna, or—

"Now we'll do it with a blindfold," he said.

Legacy stared.

"But—"

47

"No buts about it," Javi said. "You know this court well enough to do these drills with your eyes closed."

And it was true. Back on court, blindfolded, she found that she could ghost without stumbling over the net or heading off into the forest just by counting her steps, feeling her body, trusting her instincts about how to return to the T, how to move back to the baseline.

She knew this court like the back of her hand, she thought to herself, with the world darkened by Javi's bandanna. Even without the benefit of vision, she could feel the grass bend under her feet. She could *hear* the grass bend under her feet.

For that matter, she could hear bees in the forest waking up, stretching their wings, and making their pollen deliveries in the dewy morning.

"Even better!" Javi called from the sideline. Legacy grinned. She knew just where he was, leaning on the net post, by the volume of his voice. And she knew that he was happy. Even though she hadn't removed the red bandanna from over her eyes, she knew that he was grinning.

"Now last stage of Operation Ghost," he called. "Gus!"

"Wait a second," Legacy said, tearing the bandanna off. "You want me to play Gus with a blindfold? No way. In case you've forgotten, he shoots *fire*balls. You can't possibly think—"

"You can do it," Javi said. "The Legacy *I* know can play Gus with her eyes closed."

Legacy swallowed. She looked at her friend. He'd given up everything to follow her here. The least she could do was try it.

Now Gus was loping out to the baseline. Legacy took one last look at him, then lifted the bandanna and tied it over her eyes once again.

For a moment, she stood on the T. There was the sound of the bees.

She took a step forward.

There was the sound of the grass underfoot.

She listened. That was Gus, over the net, getting ready to spit out his first shot.

She bent her knees. She swayed back and forth. She felt her feet. She paid attention to her toes. She became aware of her hands, her shoulders, her neck. She acknowledged her ears, and she *listened*.

Gus shot one fireball after another, at all angles, and at a variety of speeds. As soon as she heard them thwack out of his mouth, Legacy was moving. She knew whether he'd spit a lob, whether he'd spit a drive or a cross-court. She could hear the ball whistling through the air. From the sound of its bounce, she knew just when to start swinging.

Now Legacy was like a whipwing: floating and swooping from shot to shot, thwacking the balls back to Gus's side. Over and over again, she hit the same shots: forehand drive, forehand cross-court, backhand drive, backhand cross-court. Just as she had been when she was ghosting, she was nothing but a body: a pair of feet, a pair of shoulders, her fingers on the grip.

Lulled by the repetition, Legacy's mind calmed. Her racket carved the air; it seemed to winnow away her distractions. After the hundredth forehand drive, she wasn't thinking about anything except the burn in her forearm, the specific angle of her slice. She was narrowing her technique down to the most specific degree: the slightest tilt of her wrist made all the difference. And her shots were pinging cleanly off her strings. She could hear that her drives were landing, one after the next, right on the baseline.

And she could hear that Javi was smiling.

CHAPTER SIX

LIGHT WANTS DARKNESS

That afternoon, Legacy, Javi, and Gus headed back out to the court. This time, they tried without the blindfold.

And—at first, at least—it went smoothly. Legacy was beginning to hope that the worst of her problems were behind her.

Javi, she said to herself, was right: something about those drills had gotten her back in her body.

They'd helped her anchor her mind.

This is how it was supposed to go, Legacy thought. This is what she was capable of. She was back in her rhythm, back in her zone. Gus's fireballs were singing through the forest air, but so were Legacy's returns. If she kept this up, soon she'd be glowing.

After playing Gus with a blindfold on, this was a breeze. Now she had *time*. Gus, in his new pampered condition, wasn't as powerful as he once was. Playing him without a blindfold was almost easy. Legacy had time to hear her own thoughts. Moving back and forth over the base-line, the soft grass giving under her feet, she told herself that she was the same player who beat Gia in the final of the nationals. The same player who used her light grana to push back against Gia's darkness.

And she could do it again. If she needed to. When she needed to.

At Capari, playing in front of a crowd, playing in front of *Silla*, finally having the chance to justify her friends' sacrifices, she'd do it again.

Thinking that, Legacy felt her arms get a little heavier. It was as though the pressure had shifted in the air: now it was thicker. It was harder to swing.

When she looked over the net at Gus, he'd gotten smaller, as though he'd backed up. As though the *baseline* had backed up.

Legacy shook her head. Not now. She didn't need this. What she needed to do was to focus on process, to keep throwing herself into these drills, because in thirteen days she'd be at Capari, and she'd be expected to beat not only Gia with her darker-than-night darkness, but also that other Legacy, that taller Legacy with stronger light grana.

The net was growing. The baseline was retreating. Legacy narrowed her eyes. Not now. Not this!

She threw herself into her swing, determined to get the ball over the net. Gus countered with a cross-court. Legacy was feeling heavier and heavier, as though the weight of the air were pressing her into the court. She couldn't afford this. Not now that Silla was looking for any excuse to destroy her.

With all her strength, she hurled herself into returning his shot. She had to get it over that enormous net. She had to get it all the way back to that distant baseline.

"Out!" Javi yelled, throwing away his reed in frustration. "Again! That's the fifth shot in a row you've hit out!"

Legacy shook her head. Javi came into focus. So did Gus, and all the balls that had landed beyond him. Now Javi was storming over to her, followed closely by Pippa, who had joined them at the court with her stringing kit, perhaps hoping to watch Legacy practice so that she could get a sense of what sorts of improvements in her stringbind might be necessary to help her play better.

Legacy felt her cheeks burning. It was almost too much to bear. To have felt as good as she felt that morning—as free, as capable, playing like that with a blindfold—and now to feel as if all that progress had been erased.

"You've got to stay in your body," Javi was saying. "Just like this morning, when you were ghosting. Just like when you were playing with that blindfold."

"Now that you can see," Pippa said, "you're thinking too much. You have to let your thoughts go."

"You have to be in your body."

"You have to—"

"Stop!" Legacy said. "Please. Not now. I can't deal with another argument about training versus meditation."

Pippa glanced at Javi. "Actually—"

Legacy gritted her teeth. She didn't like how her eyes were starting to swim with tears. "What did I say, Pippa?" she said, hoping she sounded angry instead of sad. "Do you think Gia has to deal with this? Do you think she has to mediate between her bickering coaches? Or that other Legacy, who apparently has such excellent grana? Does she have to make corn porridge for a house full of littles?"

Pippa glanced at Javi again. Javi glanced back at Pippa.

"Actually," Pippa said again, "what I was going to say is that I think Javi's right. Maybe this *is* about process. I was reading up on it last night. It's a kind of physical meditation. Think of it as a synthesis of meditation and movement. Instead of sitting and breathing, you're moving and breathing. Focusing on each step and each angle. The weight of the racket, the bounce of the ball."

Javi nodded. "Exactly. Sweat and reps. Just like this morning, when you played with the blindfold. It's pushing yourself to the furthest physical limit so you don't have time or space for these thoughts about whether or not you can beat Gia. Or that other girl, that other Legacy. The key is setting yourself up against an opponent who will push you to that limit, and then playing that opponent over and over again—" Javi stopped, interrupted by the sound of laughter.

Zaza and some of the other littles had made their way to the court, and were now feeding Gus so many honey cakes that honey was dribbling down his chest. He was lying on his back on the court, hooves up in the air, and Zaza had started scratching his belly.

Javi sighed. "What we're saying is—"

"We know how much you love Gus," Pippa interrupted. "We all love Gus! But the truth about pyruses is that they don't have the creativity of real players."

"And let's be honest," Javi said. "This one's lost some of his edge."

"His fireballs are a little soft," Pippa said.

"Maybe that's why you're hitting everything long," Javi said.

Pippa nodded. "We're saying that we think you need a stronger opponent."

Legacy glanced over at Gus. Just thinking about replacing him made her feel guilty.

"I don't know," she said. "I think maybe it's all in my head. I keep seeing the net grow. And the baseline retreat. And—"

Now the littles had made a makeshift baby carriage out of a

wheelbarrow. They'd somehow lured Gus to climb inside, and they were wheeling him around like a baby.

She sighed. "Maybe you're right," she said.

"Even if it *is* in your head," Pippa said, "that's the whole point: we're trying to get you *out* of your head."

"Out of your head and onto the court," Javi said.

"And that's why you need a stronger opponent. The challenge of playing Gus with the blindfold on got you to stop thinking. With the blindfold off, it wasn't enough of a challenge."

"But where am I going to find another opponent?" Legacy said. "I can't go back to the academy. Silla won't let me."

Pippa nodded. "We know. That's why we were thinking—is there anyone else? Any players you could compete against in the provinces?"

"Because if you're going to compete against Gia's darkness," Javi said, pointing to a copy of the *Nova Times* that he'd pulled out of his pocket, "you're going to need to be on top of your game."

Pippa elbowed Javi and gave him a smoldering glare, but somehow he missed it.

"Because, I mean, if this article is true," he went on, "her darkness is unreal. I mean, it's going to be the deepest darkness you've ever seen. Way deeper than the darkness when you played her at nationals."

Legacy felt a cold sweat spreading over her brow. The darkness Gia had at the nationals was bad enough. The bats flying out from under the ramparts, the shadows that deepened and deepened until it seemed to Legacy as though she'd be lost in them forever.

Pippa was desperately elbowing Javi, but he was still going on. "It's gonna be darker than anything you've ever imagined, darker than the old mines of Minori, the ones they don't use anymore because they've stripped them clean. It'll be darkness like the darkness that's supposed to settle in the deepest, untapped mineral caverns—"

"So why don't we go there!" Legacy shouted, mostly as a way to stop Javi from talking more. "Let's go to Minori. Let's go see that darkness. Let's get away from all of these distractions and go train in the kind of darkness that I'll have to eventually play in."

It had started as a way of interrupting Javi, but as she talked, Legacy found herself warming to the idea. That feeling she'd had this morning, ghosting with the blindfold on: it was the most exhilarating feeling she'd had in a long time. Maybe the most exhilarating feeling she'd had since she left for the academy. And if Minori was where she had to go to recapture that feeling, well, Minori it was.

And then she remembered—Jenni Bruno lived in Minori.

"The best tennis player I competed against, besides Gia, is down there. She didn't even have grana, but her intensity, her strength, her love for the game: it was incredible. She'd be the perfect training partner, a real change of routine, and—"

"And we can get some prosite there!" Pippa said. Javi and Legacy looked at her.

"Prosite?" Javi said.

"The mineral connected to process," Pippa said. "We didn't bring any from the academy, and I've been out, and when I was reading up on it last night, I saw something about needing to add more prosite to a player's stringbind as she becomes more experienced. As pressure starts to build, and she becomes fearful. Then in order to balance the stringbind's metium, it's important to add prosite, to help the player connect to the basic processes of training."

"Then it's decided!" Legacy said. "We'll go to Minori, where I can train against Jenni Bruno and get some practice with darkness."

"And I'll pick up some prosite!" Pippa added.

Legacy laughed. "We will get you as much prosite as your heart desires," she said.

Both of them looked at Javi, expecting him to be excited, but he'd grown somewhat ashen and was now shifting nervously from one sneaker to the next.

"I don't know," he said, chewing the inside of his cheek. "I mean, at the end of the day, it's just reps and sweat—"

"You've said it yourself," Legacy said. "I've been distracted. I need a stronger training partner. And it wouldn't hurt to have a change of routine. And . . . and maybe seeing that darkness will be the thing I need to really trigger my grana. Maybe light *wants* darkness."

Pippa nodded eagerly, but Javi still seemed skeptical. He was still chewing the inside of his cheek. His hands seemed empty without a reed. Watching his face, Legacy remembered the lengths to which he'd gone to get out of Minori. The mining province was where his family had been banished to after his father had been accused of theft. There, he'd lived in exile, desperate to prove his worth in the city. Then he'd gotten out. He'd found a way. And now she and Pippa were asking him to go back.

But it was a good plan. Even he saw that. And now, finally, he shrugged and seemed to relent. "Well, I guess there's plenty of heavy stuff you can lift there," he said. "And if darkness is what you want— sure. Minori's the darkest place imaginable."

CHAPTER SEVEN

THE HIGH CRIME
OF FAKERY

Early the next morning, Legacy paused outside her father's door. She hated goodbyes, even if it would just be a few days. And what if he told her she couldn't go? His words, after she came back from the city last time, still echoed in her head: "If you disobey me again—"

Maybe, she thought, a note would be best. But she'd snuck off last time, and the guilt of it! She couldn't do that again. She didn't want him to be unprepared for her absence. Swallowing the knot that had formed in her throat, Legacy pushed open the door.

Her father was still in bed. He looked up at her from where he lay, propped up on a pillow, and before he could admonish her for coming in without knocking, a coughing fit interrupted him.

Legacy waited until he'd gotten it under control. Then she took a deep breath. "Papa," she said. "I wanted to know—"

He shook his head wearily. "No, Legacy. No. Wherever it is— no. I can't spare you. The day you took to go to the carnival was hard enough. I've had this cold, and Hugo and Ink are too small to care for the other littles alone."

Legacy looked down at her sneakers. She knew Hugo and Ink were too small to be given so much responsibility.

But then Legacy remembered that stand at the carnival: the man hawking jobs in the mines. And Javi telling them about the toxic fumes, the unsafe conditions for miners. She didn't want Ink and Hugo to grow up too fast, but she also didn't want them to end up in the mines.

"Papa," she said, "I have to. For all of us. If I'm going to play in Capari, I have to go to Minori to train with Jenni Bruno. I can't keep training here, alone, with no one to compete against except Gus. And if I'm going to face Gia's darkness again—"

"Why?" her father said, looking angry. "Why should you have to face Gia's darkness again? Why should you have to play in Capari? You have responsibilities here. You have responsibilities to the littles—"

"I know!" Legacy said, interrupting her father. "That's why I want to go! We can look after them until they leave the orphanage, but what then? With the provinces in the state they're in, their only opportunities will be to go work in the mines, and I won't have that. I just won't. If I win at Capari, I'll be able to speak up for the provinces. I'll be able to let people know that Silla's mines are dangerous. That we need money to rebuild from the Great Fire. That what's happening here in the provinces isn't right!"

From his place in the bed, her father stared at her. It was clear that he didn't know what to say. She was right, but so was he. It was an impossible situation.

Finally, he sighed. His face had lost some of its color. There were deep lines in his forehead. He looked years older than he had when she first left for the city. "Be careful, Legacy," he said. "Minori can be a dangerous place."

"I know," Legacy said, moving forward to kiss her father on the forehead. "I know. And that's exactly why I have to go there."

At the front gate, Legacy glanced back at the orphanage. She wanted to get going before the littles woke from their naps. It had been hard enough saying goodbye to Gus.

Stroking his nose, explaining that they were going away, Legacy could tell that he wanted to come with them. But technically, Gus was an illegal pyrus; he was supposed to be back at the academy with the others that Silla had imported. He seemed safe enough here at the orphanage, miles away from the nearest settlement. And the forest near the orphanage had healed enough that the owls were coming back, frightening away Silla's crackles, those winged creatures acting as her spies. But Legacy knew that they couldn't bring him tromping through the provinces, out in the open and away from the healthiest patch of the forest.

So it was just the three of them—Legacy, Javi, and Pippa—setting off down the long drive, then turning onto the main cart road. The plan was to walk until a cart passed, at which point they could catch a ride to Minori. When they heard the first cart rattling behind them, they got off the road and stood single file while Legacy waved at the little old woman sitting up front holding the reins. She stopped her horses and smiled warmly down at the three young travelers.

Warmly, that is, until she saw Legacy up close. Then her eyes widened in her wrinkled face. "But—" she stammered, "but—haven't you seen the decree?"

Legacy smiled cheerfully. "What decree, ma'am? We're just on our way to Minori—"

The woman's face became hard. "No room," she said. "No room. No room for . . . *copycats*. There's only one Legacy Petrin!"

Confused, the three friends trod on until the clopping sound of horse hooves warned them of the approach of another cart. Once again, they stepped aside. And once again, the cart slowed until the driver caught a better look at Legacy's face. Then, shaking his head in disapproval, he clucked at his horses, and they sped off.

The next driver, at least, was kind enough to stop and offer an explanation. "Look, kids," he said. "I know it's fun to dress up as champions, but look at it from her perspective. She takes the time out of training to come out to the provinces and promote Silla's policies, and she sees a thousand imitation Legacys. How can that feel? Don't you think it would be a little alarming? We can't do that to our Legacy."

Legacy was so frustrated she stomped her foot like an annoyed child. "But I'm not dressing up!" she said. "I *am* Legacy."

The driver sighed. "Let's not be irrational," he said. "We don't have—"

Now even Pippa was getting frustrated. "She *is* Legacy. That's Legacy Petrin!"

Finally, the driver's face hardened. "It's people like you who ruin it for the rest of us," he said. "We finally have a champion. Someone who can speak for us. And you kids are out breaking decrees, making the provinces look bad. It's enough to make me want to report you to Silla's police."

Then he clucked at his horses as well, and the three friends watched the dust roll around the back wheels of his cart. By the time the fifth cart had passed them by, it was nearly lunchtime. Javi was muttering about losing a full day of training. Pippa was complaining about a blister that was forming on her heel, and about how she was hungry, and about how the humidity was affecting her curls, and Legacy had just about lost it.

"But what's this decree?" she said. "Even if these people don't believe that I'm the real Legacy, what would be so bad about me pretending to be her? Just the other day, at the carnival, half the people we saw were dressed up as me."

"I don't know," Pippa said. "I can't think straight. I'm too thirsty."

"If we don't get a ride," Javi said, "we won't get to Minori until tomorrow night. That's *two* whole days of missed training, and Capari's barely more than a week away."

"I mean, half of them looked more like me than me," Legacy said. "And I definitely saw a few better-looking Legacys."

Pippa moaned. "Didn't you hear me when I said I was thirsty?"

"What happened to your water bottle?" Legacy said.

"I never had one," Pippa grumbled. "This morning when I meant to grab my pack full of water and food, I must have accidentally grabbed my carnival pack. It's full of extra costumes, nothing of any use for the longest, most brutal hike in the universe."

"Well, it's not our fault you took the wrong pack," Javi said, glaring at Pippa. "And if we loiter, it might end up being three days of missed training."

Legacy peered toward the road. "There's a water station up ahead," she said. "I'm thirsty, too. We'll stop there for a quick break, but then we'll have to keep heading in the direction of Minori."

Legacy had never tasted such delicious water before. Once Pippa had finished guzzling, Legacy leaned over the stone trough. Placing her mouth under the O of the tap, letting the clear forest water pour into her mouth, Legacy thought that she'd miss the smell of cycapress leaves when they got to Minori. She moved aside to let Javi drink, and it was then, waiting for Javi to finish guzzling, that she saw the poster pinned over the trough.

There it was: her own face smiling down on the water. She was standing beside Silla, grinning, and they were surrounded by kids who—to judge from their burlap—came from the provinces.

LEGACY PETRIN PROVINCIAL TOUR!
COME SEE THE CHAMP!
SEE THE MIGHTY SWING! THE UNFLAPPABLE SPIRIT!
AND LEARN ABOUT A GREAT NEW
JOB OPPORTUNITY IN MINORI!

Pippa had straightened up. Now she furrowed her brow. "She's doing a publicity tour? For what?"

"What's she won?!" Legacy said, ripping the poster down off the wall.

"Well, the national championship, technically," Javi replied.

"*Not* 'technically.' *She* hasn't won *anything*."

"Come on," Javi said. "I know an inn that's a few miles on. If we hurry, we can still get there today."

Javi led the way. As they walked on the trade road, more and more carts passed. At least the drivers left them alone now that they didn't draw attention to themselves.

Legacy removed her backpack and took out an emergency pouch of corn porridge. She'd mixed it early that morning. Now, out on the road, the taste of it reminded her of home. For a moment, the anxiety of the day faded away. She was out on a hike with her friends. The sun was shining. The blue wazoons were chasing one another from branch to branch, and the kweefruits were plumping in their bushes, and—

WHOOOOSH!

Legacy stumbled into the ditch lining the road. Pippa and Javi had tumbled down here, too. From their place by the side of the road, they watched a small, gleaming black cart rush by, pulled by what looked like a pure white pyrus.

Just beyond them, at another water station, the cart came to a screeching halt. The pyrus reared up on its hind legs, snorting fire, and out jumped two of Silla's police officers. Both looked particularly short underneath two extremely tall hats. They grabbed a young woman from the water station and led her back to the cart. From her place in the ditch, Legacy stared. It wasn't just any young woman.

It was her! It was False Legacy.

She had Legacy's same long, curly hair. Her skin was the same coppery brown as Legacy's. She wore Legacy's burlap dress and Legacy's sneakers, and in her hands she clutched Legacy's racket.

Legacy felt fury rising up in her throat. She moved to leap out of the ditch—this was her chance to confront her!—until she felt Javi's and Pippa's hands pulling her backward.

"Wait," Pippa whispered.

"Look!" Javi said.

The two policemen had handcuffed the other Legacy and shoved her into the back of the cart, where she now sat, facing Legacy, Javi, and Pippa, with tears rolling down her dusty cheeks.

And from this angle, it was clear that this wasn't False Legacy at all. This wasn't the girl on the posters or in the brochure. It was . . . another one.

She was younger than False Legacy, and her dress wasn't quite right. It was too long, hanging over her knees. And while the dress was too long, her hair was too short. And her eyes: they weren't brown, like Legacy's. They were a sort of pale greenish blue.

Legacy felt pity beginning to well in her chest. The girl was sobbing now, her tears leaving glistening streaks in the makeup she'd used on her cheeks. Her shoulders—shaking under her burlap dress—were very thin, and Legacy realized that she was much younger than Legacy herself. This Legacy was maybe ten years old, and now she was getting carted off by Silla's police.

Standing beside the little cart, one of the policemen was screaming in a near falsetto voice. He seemed to want to be heard by the whole province. "On behalf of High Consul Silla," he piped, "we arrest you for the high crime of fakery!"

His partner continued. "Fakery is a criminal offense!"

"Especially faking the identity of a national champion!"

Crouching beside Pippa and Javi, Legacy watched as the police climbed back into the cart and sped off, her look-alike—still crying, clutching her racket as though it were a beloved doll—jolting up and down in the back.

Legacy felt sick to her stomach. Only two days ago, hundreds of provis had been dressed up as her. And why, today, was a little girl getting arrested for doing the exact same thing?

"I'm so confused," Pippa murmured.

"There seems to have been some sort of decree," Javi said. "Something about not imitating Legacy?"

"Not imitating *that* Legacy," Legacy said.

Pippa looked at her with big, frightened eyes. "But you!" she said. "You look like you're imitating Legacy."

"I *am* Legacy!"

"I don't understand," Pippa said. "Why would Silla have passed such a law?"

Javi pulled a reed from the side of the ditch and started chewing it. "Maybe she wants an excuse to arrest the real Legacy," he said.

"Or maybe she wants to keep me from traveling to Minori. Maybe she doesn't want me to have the chance to train in the darkness. Maybe she thinks if I can't train, I won't be able to perform well at Capari."

Pippa glanced at Javi, and Legacy almost thought she saw a sign pass between them.

"What?" she said.

Pippa reddened.

Javi shrugged. "All I know is, I don't want to be caught traveling with an imitation Legacy."

Legacy groaned. "But I'm not an imitation Legacy!"

"I know that, and Pippa knows that, but nobody else does."

"He's right," Pippa said. "If you got arrested here, nobody would know that you're the real Legacy."

"And we can't risk that," Javi said. "If you got arrested, we'd waste at *least* three precious training days before Capari."

Pippa was already pulling clothes out of her satchel. "We'll have to braid your hair," she said. "And use some paint—"

Legacy grinned. Even Javi had to nod with approval, and by the time the three friends climbed out of the ditch, they were in costume.

Legacy wore a bright blue jumpsuit with blue paint around her eyes. Her hair was coiled in two braids on the top of her head like a giraffe's "horns." Javi was wearing all yellow, with a yellow cap pulled down low over his eyes. And Pippa—well, Pippa was dressed as a fabulous cat.

"Don't you think people will find it a little strange that you're walking around the provinces in a costume?" Javi said, looking skeptically at her whiskers.

65

Pippa flushed, and Legacy stuck up for her. "You see it all the time in Cora," Legacy said. "A day, even two after the summer carnival. Sometimes people just don't want to let go of their costumes."

Pippa brightened. "I'll just wear it until we get somewhere with some quality fabric. Then I can make us all better costumes."

And so they headed off down the road, in the direction of the inn Javi had told them about: a fabulous cat, a boy dressed in yellow, and a girl dressed in blue who looked a little bit like Legacy Petrin.

While they plodded along, hoping to get to the inn before dinner, Legacy tried not to think about that little girl in the back of the police cart. She'd been so young. And now she was heading off to jail in the city.

If impersonating her had become a crime, Legacy thought, there must be others as well. Other little Legacys, wandering around the provinces, risking getting arrested just like that little Legacy. And was that her fault? Was she responsible for all those arrested Legacys? And what if she got arrested for impersonating herself? Then they'd never make it to Minori, let alone the tournament at Capari.

Legacy kept her face down. When carts passed, she felt grateful for the fading daylight. They were still walking when the sun slipped beyond the horizon and the last light turned into darkness. Then bats began to swoop overhead, and Legacy remembered playing against Gia's darkness.

And now Gia's darkness was darker than ever. Darker than the darkest night. Darker than any darkness she'd previously imagined.

Legacy swallowed. She told herself not to worry. That's why they were heading to Minori: so she could get practice with just that kind of darkness.

66

She glanced at Javi, trudging along ahead of her. "Hey, Jav," she said. "What's it like?"

"What's what like?" he said.

"Just—Minori. What was it like when you lived there?"

Javi sighed. "I don't know," he said. "It's . . . it's a glum place. Sometimes the sun barely comes out because of the big clouds of mineral dust. They blot out the sky. Then it's like you live inside of a big clump of ash."

He fell silent and touched the scar on his neck. He never talked much about it, but Legacy knew he'd been branded along with his family when his father was accused of theft.

"On the other hand," he picked up again, "in Minori, there are a lot of people like me. Exiles, thieves, children of thieves. Innocent people accused of being thieves. Desperate people accused of being thieves, and their immediate families. Mino's full of people who share my history. Back in the day, when they were trying to clean up the city, if you so much as loitered too long on a street corner, you got charged with thievery and sent to Minori to work in the mines. We all had the same brands. We even took some pride in them: at least we didn't wear city silks. There was a nice camaraderie. I had some really good buddies. Take Illy and Horzst—we used to train together. You've never known two more trustworthy, down-to-earth guys."

They walked for a moment longer in silence. Then Javi piped up again. "And, you know, on some days, when the ash settles and the sun hits the mineral blocks—well, it can be really pretty. And you know what? The food is really terrific. I know, I know—it doesn't seem real. On one hand, there's not much to eat there. But that just means that what we *do* have to work with, we make *very* tasty. In Minori, it's all about pepperfish. They're drawn from Minori Lake, which is just about the only clean place left in the province. And it's the tastiest fish on the planet. You can make roast pepperfish, smoked pepperfish, pepperfish stew, pepperfish platter, pepperfish stir-fried in butter—"

Legacy watched him musing on and on about pepperfish. It made her smile: he looked sort of goofy and boyish in a way he almost never did.

Then, however, his face changed completely. His grin disappeared.

"What?" Legacy said. "Javi, what is it?"

"Just—even if the food is really good, it's not a safe place. People get injured in the mines all the time. My friend Horzst—he wanted to be a builder, like me. Me and Horzst and Illy used to train one another after working the mines. One day Horzst fell on his way out of the cavern, and—well, that was the end of his chances of becoming an academy builder. But at least he got out. Sometimes people die in there. They go down to do a day's work, and they never come back."

Legacy shuddered. She thought again of the man hawking jobs at the summer carnival. Of Ink and little Hugo, who was only comfortable in the kitchen.

Javi looked at Legacy. "Minori is a place where you cannot forget why it's important to stay focused," he said. "One wrong move in the mines, and you never get out."

"I get it, Javi," Legacy said.

"This won't just be practice," Javi said. "This won't be a drill."

"I *get* it, Javi."

"There's no such thing as drills in Minori."

CHAPTER EIGHT

SHAPES IN THE SNOW

The inn was a sprawling old house with a green roof that dipped down so low it nearly touched the ground, where tall wispy scissor grass rose up to meet it. It gave the impression of a hill with windows, a homey little hill with windows of all sizes, out of which streamed lemon-yellow light.

Once Pippa had bartered with the innkeeper for two little rooms without windows, they dropped their bags by their beds. Pippa wanted to make better disguises—Legacy, after all, still looked like Legacy, only with giraffe braids, and much bluer than usual—but Legacy and Javi were famished, so the three friends decided to risk the dining room in their makeshift disguises.

It didn't work.

The first person who recognized her was the waiter. "Oh—oh my!" he stammered. "Welcome back, welcome back!"

Legacy stared. *Back?*

Pippa nudged her. "He thinks you're *her.*"

Her. The other Legacy Petrin.

In the waiter's haste to fill up her water, he knocked over the glass, then nearly attacked her with a napkin, and finally ran off in a state of near tears.

The manager of the inn came out in his wake. "Ms. Petrin! Ms. Petrin. We have been eagerly anticipating your charity tour, and here you are at our humble inn! What an honor, what an absolute, unexpected honor. Here, let me get you a dry table—"

Legacy paused. The other Legacy was traveling through on her "tour" of the provinces. Should Legacy clarify that she wasn't the same person? How strange, to feel like an impersonator of herself.

Beside her, Pippa was eyeing the fresh bread rolls on the new table. Javi's stomach audibly growled. Legacy sighed and followed the manager to their new table.

As the three of them wound their way through the dinner crowd, heads turned. Children whispered in their parents' ears, and some bold people reached out just to touch Legacy's shoulder. She'd never experienced this kind of adoration. It gave her a little thrill, and yet, at the same time, she was plagued by the feeling that the person they imagined they were adoring wasn't her. Or *was* her, but not—

"Aren't you going to say something?" Pippa whispered urgently in her ear as they sat down at a private table in the back.

"Like what? That the Legacy Petrin they all love is a fake? Didn't you see what happened to that girl this afternoon? Do you want me to be arrested for . . . being myself?"

They didn't have to order anything. The food just came. Wave after wave of it, delivered by a small army of waiters. Javi adapted to the attention quickly.

"Maybe some spicy mustard, too, please," he asked a waiter as though he were used to being waited on hand and foot. The waiter bowed and rushed off to the kitchen. "And maybe a platter of the best cheese you keep in the kitchen?"

Pippa rolled her eyes. "Very gauche, Javi," she said.

Legacy nearly laughed, then recalled that though Pippa had probably eaten at many of the best restaurants in the city, this might have been Javi's first time. Then she sighed. She pushed her plate away and rested her head in her hands. She wished she were back in the simple dining room at home, surrounded by misbehaving littles.

"Um, Ms. Petrin—"

Legacy looked up at the hopeful face of a boy with round cheeks and black hair and big, earnest brown eyes.

"Legacy," she said. "Please call me Legacy."

She could see two adults were standing a few feet behind him, smiling. They were obviously his parents.

"I just wanted to say," the boy said, "that you've been such an inspiration. Your . . . everything. How hard you play, and the fact that you come from the provinces, like me. And your generosity . . ." He blushed and turned, but his parents whispered encouragement. "I just know that here in Cora, we're all very certain that one day you'll make as good a leader as you are a tennis player."

Legacy stared. A leader? The thought had never occurred to her. It was true that many of the best tennis players rose to positions of political power. They were often sponsored by senators or powerful businesspeople in the city; sponsoring a successful player was an excellent way to gain public support. And in exchange, those sponsors often offered top players apprenticeships in their offices, which served as launching pads for impressive careers.

But Legacy was just a kid from the provinces. She'd won one national championship. She wasn't sure she'd ever win another tournament.

Still, however, this boy seemed to believe in her.

After he left, another came. Then a girl. Then two girls, twins. Almost the entire inn came by to tell her how much they believed in her. That they were inspired by her, grateful to her, that they hoped one day she'd rise to a position of leadership in the nation.

"Wow," Pippa said, yawning. "People really love this other Legacy. She must be pretty inspirational."

Legacy turned, ready to snap at her friend. But she was right. It wasn't her they were inspired by: it was False Legacy. The one who was touring the provinces, whose exhibition matches these kids had seen, whose light they were all so impressed by. These kids weren't thanking her. They were thanking False Legacy.

It was late by the time Legacy asked for the check. "No, no," the waiter said, backing away from her as though he was afraid she might lash out. "Your presence is payment enough. And good luck tomorrow."

Legacy nodded but stole a look at Javi and Pippa. They looked as confused as she was. "Yes," she said. "Thank you. I'll need all the luck I can get to . . . um—"

The waiter smiled. "Villy Sal is very talented, and we've heard so much about the blizzards he's able to conjure. So you can imagine how excited we all are to come see your exhibition against him at the fairgrounds tomorrow. Normally, two such excellent players wouldn't ever come out to the provinces, but of course you're changing all that, Ms. Petrin!"

Back in Legacy and Pippa's room, the kids held a quick meeting.

"We should go," Javi said. "We'll just stay a few hours, and it'll be a chance to scout out the competition. Like I've always said, 'you can't win if you don't know what you're competing against.'"

Legacy looked at him. "The competition? I thought Gia was the competition. I thought False Legacy was a distraction."

Javi looked at Pippa. Pippa looked down.

"Out with it!" Legacy snapped. "Ever since we left, whenever False Legacy comes up, it's clear that you two are hiding something."

Pippa sighed. "You're right. It's just—we were trying to figure out how to tell you. Before we left, I tried to register you for Capari. Turns out, you were already registered. Or Legacy Petrin was already registered."

It took a moment for Legacy to understand. Then her stomach sank. "She's registered in my place."

Pippa nodded. "So if we are going to register," Pippa said, "if you are going to play, you'll have to do it under a false name. And you'll have to play in disguise."

Legacy nodded slowly. Her face felt cold. She felt as though she'd been slapped.

"And we can do that," Pippa said. "But you should be aware that it's pretty likely that at some point in the tournament, you'll have to play—"

"Her," Legacy whispered.

"So she is the competition," Javi said. "Which means it might be worth the risk to go watch her. See how strong she really is. See if she has any weaknesses."

"I don't know," Legacy said. "It's such a risk. What if I get seen? What if we get arrested? What if that's the plan—lure us out into the open with the promise of an exhibition?"

"I think it's worth it," Javi said.

"And you, Pippa?"

73

Pippa bit the side of her thumbnail. "Well—the thing is, normally I'd say yes, but, well, I've been doing some research. And there are these strange paragraphs in the old books about players having to face off against players who look like them and have similar grana. In the books, they're called 'doubles,' and the situation seems to involve some sort of danger."

Javi looked skeptical. "Those old fables? Those were all fictions. Metaphors, or something like that. Not historical truth. We learned about it at the academy."

"Maybe," Pippa said. "But what if there was a kernel of truth? I don't know, but it worries me a little bit. I think if we could see her, if we could see the differences between her and Legacy, it might set my mind at ease."

Now Javi was back on board. "Sure," he said. "Scout out the competition. It's like I've always said: you can't train unless you know what you're training for."

Legacy sighed. "Well, we can't go in these costumes."

Pippa nodded. "You're right. It took about two seconds for everyone in that dining room to think that you were Legacy."

Legacy felt a moment of irritation: they didn't *think* that she was Legacy. She *was* Legacy. But then she remembered that little girl getting carted off by the police.

"Pippa," she said, "do you think you could sew us some really good costumes?"

Pippa wasn't convinced. "I have scissors and needles, but what about fabric?"

Legacy glanced at the white sheets on the beds. "Maybe we could . . . borrow these?"

Javi shook his head. "And *I'm* the one who's supposed to be a thief."

He dug into his pocket and found a few coins, which he placed on the bedside table. "This should cover the cost of replacing them."

Legacy smiled, and Pippa got out her sewing needle.

———

Swept up in the crowd, their disguises worked like a charm. Javi was wearing a white bedding cap and a billowy white shirt made out of a pillowcase. Legacy's and Pippa's hair had been braided into coils at the napes of their necks and covered in strips of white bedding. The white collars of their gowns were so high that they covered their mouths.

If anything, they looked like three members of an odd clique, but the crowd was too excited to see Villy Sal and False Legacy to pay them any mind. There were police at all the entrances, presumably keeping an eye out for imitation Legacys, but Legacy kept her face down, and no one stopped the three kids on their way in to their seats.

Despite the weirdness and eeriness of the occasion, Legacy couldn't help but feel a thrill. It had only been a day since she'd seen a tennis court, but even the short time away had refilled her love of the game. Little cloud shadows flitted across the green grass of the court. The white lines were crisp and resplendent in the sun. And Legacy Petrin looked strong and ready, walking to her bench in her trademark burlap, with a Tempest bag slung over her shoulder—

Legacy blinked.

Javi elbowed her.

Pippa pointed.

It was *her*.

"That's . . . that's really freaky," Pippa said. "There's no other word for it."

"She's a dead ringer," Javi said, leaning forward and shielding his eyes with his hands.

Pippa breathed something about the books being right.

Legacy furrowed her brow. "What do you mean?"

But before Pippa could answer, Javi had grabbed Legacy's elbow. "That's *you* down there! How did Silla do that?"

Everyone around them was cheering for Legacy. From her bench, she smiled and waved in all directions. She looked poised, radiant, *ready*.

"Wow," Javi said. "She's pretty impressive."

Pippa nodded. She was trying to chew her thumbnail, but the high collar of her costume kept getting in the way. "She's so charismatic. And *beautiful*. Just like the books say. A very beautiful Legacy."

The crowd seemed to agree. They were cheering in adoration, until suddenly the energy changed. There were boos and shouts. Villy had arrived, with his gleaming black pompadour and his implacable expression, and though they might have loved him in the city, out here in the provinces, he wasn't the favorite.

Watching him stride out onto the baseline, Legacy was impressed. He looked strong. Stronger than he had when she played against him in the semifinals of the national championships.

Preparing to serve, he bounced the ball on the baseline: once, twice. When he looked up, his face was very pale. When he tossed the ball to serve, it was as though he was signaling to the sky.

Suddenly the clouds began to lower. They grew opaque. And by the time Villy had swung over the serve, snow was flurrying down. One minute it had been a warm summer day in Cora. The next it was snowing.

As Villy continued to play—he was dominating False Legacy in the first game of the set, pinning her to the baseline with hard drive after hard drive—Legacy began to see shapes in the snow. First it was luminous shreds, like white ribbons dancing over the court. But then those shreds started to combine. They congealed into forms that danced between Villy and False Legacy, like shadow players engaged in their own shadow match.

Pippa breathed. "They look like ghosts," she said.

Javi's mouth was hanging open. "It's like those shapes people were talking about in Gia's darkness: 'A darkness so dark even people in the crowd start to have nightmares.'"

Legacy just stared. The shapes in the snow: they were people Legacy knew but couldn't quite place. They were playing tennis, drinking water on the sidelines, talking with one another. Chattering, laughing, accusing. One of the apparitions looked like Van. It *was* Van. Legacy leaned forward. Van! She had forgotten how much she missed him: his sweet smile, the way his glasses were always crooked, the way he knew what she was thinking even before she'd said a word . . .

Now he looked up at her in the stands: "You're not like her," he said. "You don't have what she has. She's better."

Then he shrugged, picked up his racket, and danced a strange little jig on the sideline. "You may have come first," he said, "but she's the better Legacy Petrin!"

Legacy felt a sharp bonk on the back of her head, and then hands on her back, steadying her. She had hit her head on the bleacher behind her, and when she opened her eyes, she could see the annoyed face of the woman behind her blotting out the sky.

Javi and Pippa lifted her back into her seat. "Are you okay?" Pippa whispered.

"I'm fine. I just . . . did you guys hear that?"

"Hear what?" Pippa said.

"I thought I heard— Oh, never mind."

"Are you sure?" Javi said.

Pippa was peering at her in concern. "Maybe we should go back to the inn. Or get on the road. We don't have to watch this."

"I'm *fine*," Legacy whispered savagely. "If I can't handle Villy's grana up here . . . how can I possibly hope to face him—let alone Gia— on court at Capari?"

Javi sat down, silent and chastened.

Legacy frowned at him. He looked away.

On court, False Legacy was switching sides. She'd lost the first game, but she seemed cheerful and composed. She smiled up at some fans in the first row. She smiled up at everyone.

"She's a very smiley Legacy," Pippa said.

Javi nodded in agreement. "She smiles more than you do, that's for darn sure."

Pippa laughed, and Legacy had to smile as well.

"Smiley Legacy," she murmured, and watched while Smiley launched a powerful serve to Villy's backhand, then moved forward to volley and began . . . radiating gold light.

Legacy felt her stomach sink.

"It's true, then," Pippa whispered.

"It's not a trick," Javi breathed.

The crowd was going wild. They loved her. They loved this glowing Legacy.

As Villy and Smiley traded points, their respective grana also battled for dominance over the net. Villy's blizzard would thicken and twirl when he lined up to hit a fierce forehand drive, snow surging over the net toward Smiley, but then it would run into a radiant wall and quickly disperse as Smiley smashed the ball back.

Smiley was strong. She was placing the ball into far corners and making Villy run around like he was still learning how to play. And the whole time, she was smiling.

They played just two sets. Villy took the first, and Smiley took the second. Legacy assumed it would be called a tie, but the crowd started chanting for Smiley, and the judge decided to award the win to Smiley.

Villy didn't seem to care much. It was just an exhibition: all part of Silla's plan. And since Silla sponsored Villy as well as False Legacy, they were both playing for the same person.

As Villy packed his rackets into his bag, the opaque snow clouds tightened into a funnel, then disappeared into the bag along with the rackets.

He walked off court, and the crowd started to settle. Smiley stepped up to a podium down in front of the bleachers and began to shout out a short victory speech. Her voice sounded, well, exactly like Legacy's.

"All credit to High Consul Silla today for this victory—she makes all things possible! Thanks to my opponent, Villy Sal, who as usual played very well; though of course, as everyone says"—and here she paused for a moment, and smiled a wry and utterly charming smile—"no one shines brighter than Legacy Petrin."

The crowd cheered. Legacy clenched her hands into fists.

"And though today we play a game, I want to acknowledge that there are more important things going on as well. I know many of you are excited about the new opportunities out here in the provinces, especially those which come from Silla's newest and grandest plans in Minori!"

The crowd cheered even louder.

"Plans that will create many new mining jobs!"

The crowd cheered.

"Mining jobs that will yield ever more prosite, and honor the great Silla with increased productivity!"

The crowd sort of cheered.

"And bring prosperity to your families!"

The crowd absolutely cheered.

Then Smiley smiled even wider and waved and stepped down from the podium. The crowd got to its feet and began to rush for the exit. There would be a meet and greet down by the concession stand.

Legacy, Pippa, and Javi followed the crowd and elbowed their way close enough to hear Smiley Legacy being interviewed by Paula Verini, whose braids were gathered into her signature complicated knot.

"So, Legacy, what other plans do you have, out here in the provinces?" Paula asked, her voice dripping with honey.

"Oh, I'm just happy to be here," Smiley said. "Happy to be back where I'm most at home. Happy to be supporting Silla's new mining policies, and happy to have a chance to visit all the old haunts!"

Legacy's nails were digging crescents into her own palms. *Happy, happy, happy*, she thought. She'd seen enough. Now she grabbed Pippa and Javi by the elbows, and the three friends headed away from the fairgrounds, toward a large crossroads, where they followed the wooden signpost that pointed in the direction of Minori. As they walked, the ground grew rockier, and the trees grew smaller and more straggly.

"That—that was *freaky*," Pippa said. Her face was as pale as one of Villy Sal's ghosts.

"I don't know what was freakier," Javi said. "Those shapes in the snow, or the fact that Silla's found someone who looks and sounds exactly like Legacy."

"And has light grana as well," Pippa said.

"Light grana even stronger than Legacy's!" Javi said, and Pippa gave him a sharp look.

Legacy felt tears beginning to prick her eyes. "He's right," she said. "Her grana was stronger than mine. And she's better, too. Did you see those drives? I can't even keep my drives in, let alone hit them with that kind of accuracy."

"I don't get it," Javi said. "Before you came along, there hadn't been a kid with light grana in years. Now there are two. And one of them looks exactly like you."

"Maybe there aren't two," Pippa said.

Legacy shook her head. "He's right, Pip. She does have light grana. And she does look exactly like me."

"No," Pippa said. "I mean maybe there aren't two kids. What if the other Legacy's fake?"

Legacy felt her impatience returning. "Pippa, she *is* fake. I'm me, remember? She can't be Legacy Petrin."

"No, no, no, I mean, like, not real. Not *human*."

Javi scowled. "If this is going to be more mumbo jumbo about fables and—"

"What if," Pippa said, "that Legacy's made out of string?"

Legacy stopped walking and faced Pippa. "What do you mean?"

"There are theories . . . Ancient Stringing Craft theories—"

Legacy could practically hear Javi's eyes rolling.

Pippa held up one hand. "Hear me out," she said. "You remember those weavings of cats in my father's workshop? String cats? And then we saw one leap to life? I wasn't sure it was real—I mean, I thought maybe we were seeing things. But what if . . . what if there's such a thing as weaving children?"

"String children?" Legacy said.

Pippa nodded. "I know it sounds impossible," she said. "But those cats—they looked just like the real thing."

Javi looked doubtful. "So you're saying that Smiley may be just some kind of . . . doll or puppet or something?" he said. "Then how come she was able to summon so much light grana? To do that, wouldn't she have to be real?"

Pippa frowned. "I don't know," she said. "We didn't study this back at the academy. And now—well, these aren't really ideal conditions for research. If I had access to a library, or even the orphanage attic— maybe then I could give you guys some clearer answers. But for now, I don't know. It's just a theory."

Legacy started walking toward Minori again, this time at double speed. "Well, whether she's some kind of puppet or not, it doesn't matter. She could be a *pyrus*, for all it matters. The world thinks she's me. And if I'm going to prove that *I'm* me, not her, I'm going to have to get my game back. 'No one shines brighter than Legacy Petrin.' Isn't that the saying? Well. If I'm going to prove that I'm Legacy Petrin, I'm going to have to show everyone in the republic that I can shine brighter than she can."

CHAPTER NINE

THE DEEPEST DARKNESS

The sun began to glow red as it sank toward the crest of a hill they were climbing. The road had been empty for hours: not a single cart they could hop. Javi kept insisting they were "basically there!" and Legacy hoped he was right. She was tired of walking. She was tired of hearing Pippa complain about her various blisters. She was tired of wasting time that could have been spent training.

"We can stay tonight with Illy and Horzst," Javi was saying. "They have a place with direct access to the mines, which is where we'll want to do most of our training."

Legacy smiled. Javi was getting more and more upbeat the closer they got to Minori. It was obvious that he was getting excited about seeing his old friends, visiting his old home. Now he scrambled ahead to the crest of the hill. Pippa—who was still complaining of blisters— muttered a mantra of resilience, and Legacy wiped the dirt from her forehead, and the two of them plodded ahead until they reached the peak and found Javi—and Minori.

The top of the hill fell away, dropping into a crater. Struck by the red light from the setting sun, the bowl of it almost seemed to be on fire. Except that on second glance, it was crammed with blocks of glinting red stone.

"The metium mine," Javi said. Beyond it, there were more craters: silver and sparkling like moondust; pink flecked with purple and brown; deep blue like some cold northern river.

All of them cut deep into the ground, terraced with blocks of carved rock and paths for the trucks to carry off what had been mined. They circled a round lake at the center, which had now begun to glimmer with starlight.

On the far hillside, beyond the pits, there were endless miners' shacks: little houses carved into the ground, with occasional windows and every so often a roof made of corrugated tin.

"These are just the aboveground pits," Javi said. "Where the less pure minerals are carved out. The pure stuff—and the dangerous stuff—is underground. Down in the metium caves and the prosite tunnels."

Legacy stared. The glistening red of the metium pits had struck her, at first, as brilliant. But now that the sun had slipped beyond the far hillside, it was a deeper, more ominous red: almost like blood. Above them, uninterrupted by trees, the sky was endless. It must have been an especially clear night, because Legacy had never seen so many stars. They glittered, cold and hard and impossibly distant.

"Home sweet home," Javi said with a dry laugh. Legacy began to say something, but a cool gust of wind blew reddish dust into her mouth. It was Pippa who led the way down the zigzagging path, which skirted the metium mine first, and then the silver prosite pit. Finally, it led up the hillside through miners' shacks.

Each one was tiny—no bigger than one of the bedrooms in the

orphanage—but the little windows glowed with candlelight, and Legacy could smell the scent of dinners being cooked over the fire. Every so often, passing an open door, you could hear the sounds of people laughing, babies crying, fathers singing lullabies. Sometimes they passed a miner on the street wearing the typical Minorian outfit: a leather cap pulled down low over the forehead and a burlap jumpsuit—long-sleeved—with buttons up the front and tabs at the waist. Sometimes, the miner looked up at them and smiled, and Legacy could see the iridescent dust that had coated their face, or sparkled on their eyelashes. There were occasional carts selling food, and people gathered at the rickety little tables and chairs that had been set out before them. Through the windows of a few taverns, Legacy could see people drinking foamy liquid out of glass cups, playing darts and table tennis.

A full moon had joined the stars overhead, and in the pale moonlight, Legacy could see that every window of every shack, every tin roof, every sign for every tavern was coated in a shimmery dust: red or silver or purple pink. The dust coated every surface: every stone on the path, every blade of grass that had managed to survive alongside it.

"Where did you live, Javi?" Legacy said.

"Where are your parents?" Pippa said.

Javi paused, then kept trudging determinedly ahead. "They live behind the somni mine," he said. "But that's not where we're going."

"Why?" Legacy said. "Don't you want to see them?"

Javi sighed. "When I left—well, we weren't on the best of terms. When we were exiled, my mother blamed my father. My father blamed my mother. My sister and I blamed them both. We did our best, I guess, but after a few years of long hours in the mines, our family just fell apart. My mother left. My father—I guess he sort of lost himself. I just focused on my dream of becoming an academy builder, and as soon as I could, I went to live with my friends Horzst and Illy."

"You don't just want to stop by?" Pippa said. "I mean, I have a blister and I'm very thirsty, but—"

"Can we not talk about it?" Javi said.

"It's just that family is family," Pippa said. A strange, stubborn look had settled over her face. Legacy remembered how Pippa's own family had sent her to live at the academy when she was just a young child. Then Pippa's father—when he had discovered them sneaking into his workshop—had all but disowned his daughter.

Now Legacy wondered whether Pippa had regrets about leaving before she'd had a chance to mend the rift between her and her family. Whether, now that there was so much distance between them, she'd remembered what she loved about them—

"Illy and Horzst are my family," Javi said.

"Well, that's nice, I guess," Pippa said, still with that stubborn look. "Now you get to reunite with them. Maybe this was all part of the plan. The universe speaking, the one great unknown giving—"

"Sure," Javi snapped, leading the way down a smaller road that led down a steep, narrow passageway between shacks. "Sure, part of the plan to become an academy builder was to actually just give up on being an academy builder and come back to the one place I wanted to leave."

Legacy winced. That, too, was her fault. "I'm sorry, Javi."

She saw his shoulders drop. He must have regretted his tone, because he trudged on in silence for a few minutes, but when he spoke next, his voice had softened.

"It's okay," he said. "I used to think the only thing that mattered was making a plan and sticking with it. But sometimes, I guess, we don't get to choose our destiny."

———————

Illy and Horzst's house—the house Javi used to share with them, once he'd moved out of his parents' place—was basically a hole dug into the ground. The door leading into it—a circular hole covered with a plank—was on the outskirts of the city, halfway between the prosite pit and the metium mine. It was surrounded by dozens of other similar doors, leading down into the ground.

Javi looked around before lifting the plank.

"There are more of these houses now," he said. "Underground houses. Houses that lead straight to the tunnels."

"Why?" Pippa said. "Wouldn't people want a little light? My mother always said, 'Light is the only furnishing more necessary for a well-appointed living room than—'"

Javi rolled his eyes. "We're not in the city anymore. Choice isn't exactly a factor here in Minori," he said. "People live here because it's easier to access the tunnels. And when you work thirteen hours a day, a long commute isn't exactly exciting."

"So Illy and Horzst work in the tunnels?" Legacy said.

Javi nodded. "I would have to," he said. "If I'd stayed here. If I hadn't gone off to the city. When I went, I had to leave them behind."

Legacy thought about Van heading off to go learn at the School of Economics. The way he'd looked over his shoulder and waved, heading down the long orphanage driveway. "You must be excited to see them."

Javi grinned. "I can't wait to see their expressions when they open the door and see me back here. These guys are the best. You're gonna love them."

"Well then, let's go down there," she said. "I'm looking forward to getting to know them."

Javi rapped on the door.

"Go away!" came a voice from inside.

"Yeah, go away!" came another, huskier voice.

Javi chuckled. "Open up, you two goons! It's Javi!"

There was a long silence. Javi glanced back at Legacy.

"Oh, how nice," came the first voice. "You deigned to come visit us from the city."

The round door in the ground remained shut.

Javi's face had fallen. Legacy felt a surge of anger on her friend's behalf.

"How kind of you," came the huskier voice, "to come down from the heights of your career!"

"And offer us the charity of—"

Legacy stepped forward and tore the plank off the hole. She was sick of this. Sick of friends forgetting their former closeness. Trying not to think about that image of Van dancing his cruel little dance, she lowered herself down into a room that had been carved out of the earth. It was furnished with two pallets on the ground, one earthen firepit with a kettle balanced on top, and about a hundred different weight-lifting contraptions.

Beyond that, Legacy couldn't see anything. The room was very dark, and her eyes hadn't adjusted yet. Still, she tried to adopt a disdainful expression. She put her hands on her hips. "I'm Legacy Petrin," she said. "And you two are being extraordinarily rude. One of your closest friends is up there, knocking on the door, and you two have the nerve—"

Two brown faces emerged from the gloom. Both shimmered with silver dust. One of the figures lit a candle, then they held it up to her face.

"You're not Legacy Petrin," said the one with the huskier voice. He was stockily built, so short his burlap jumpsuit was rolled to a thick cuff at his ankles, one of which was ringed with thick scars. Legacy remembered what Javi had said about his old friend's injury.

"Why would Legacy Petrin end up in our house?" the other one said. He was taller and thinner and seemed to be a few years older. He wore a leather cap pulled over his eyebrows. His patchy beard seemed to have been black at one point, but now it shimmered with silver dust.

The short one laughed. It was not a happy laugh. "Think of it, Illy," he said. "The great Legacy Petrin, Silla's stooge, ending up in our house—"

Legacy heard two thuds behind her.

"She's not Silla's stooge," Pippa said, her voice filtering through the darkness.

"And this isn't just your house," Javi said. "I put down half of the deposit, back when we were roommates, and we're staying here as long as we decide to train in Minori."

The tall one—Illy—looked like he was about to protest, but Legacy stepped in.

"Just a couple of days," she said. "Before we head back to the forest."

The short one—Horzst—had come closer, holding the candle up to her face.

"You're really her, aren't you?" he said.

Legacy nodded.

"Somehow I thought you'd be a little taller," he said.

Legacy narrowed her eyes and Horzst backed off a bit.

"Okay," he said. "So you're Legacy Petrin. Well. I have to say. I went to the city and saw you play Gia. It was pretty good. We were all . . . well, we were all pretty impressed with your performance that day."

The tall one nodded. "Politics aside, you might even say that we were inspired."

"Thanks," Legacy said. "It was all because of Javi. Javi and Pippa. My friends."

The two kids gave Javi a look of grudging respect.

Javi shrugged. "I want to train her down in the tunnels," he said.

"Don't you have access to the greatest gyms in the country?" Horzst said.

"We've heard all about the whirlpools, and the silk resistance mechanisms, and—"

"Not anymore," Pippa said.

"We left," Javi said.

Legacy nodded. "We're training in the provinces."

Illy and Horzst still looked skeptical.

"We're training *for* the provinces," Legacy said.

Illy shook his head. "That's not true. Just this morning, I read in the papers about a Legacy Petrin charity tour, and how she's sponsored by Silla—"

"That's fake," Legacy said.

"She's not really Legacy," Pippa said.

Illy and Horzst glanced at each other, as though trying to decide whether the other one was buying it.

"It's a long story," Javi said. "But I swear on my pickax: that other girl, the one on the 'charity tour,' she's not really Legacy. *This* is Legacy. She's not Silla's stooge. She's the first champion from the provinces. We're going to prove that. But if we're going to do it, I need to train her down in the tunnels. We're looking for Jenni Bruno. And some prosite dust. And we want her to train in real darkness."

Illy leaned forward and whispered something in Horzst's ear. Then the two of them glanced at a third pallet that had been propped up against the wall and used as a dartboard.

Then Horzst stepped forward. He was looking at Javi. "We didn't like the way you left without looking back. The way you never came and visited us when you moved to the city. But I guess you're here now, and now's better than never." He extended his hand to Javi.

Legacy was surprised to feel her eyes getting wet. If only she could see Van. If only she could ask him why he hadn't responded to her letters. Then maybe she could shake the memory of that wraith dancing that horrible jig. Then maybe she'd feel like herself again, the self she knew she was because Van knew her also.

Even Javi must have been touched by the gesture, because for a moment he stood very still with his hand covering his face. When he finally stepped forward and shook Horzst's hand, his expression was as grave as Legacy had ever seen it. "I should have been in touch," he said. "I don't know why I didn't. I just—I forgot myself. That's the only way I can describe it. I forgot myself for a minute."

For a moment, the two friends somberly shook hands before Horzst pulled Javi closer and hugged him.

"On my pickax," Illy was muttering, wiping a tear away from his eyes.

Javi extricated himself from Horzst and hugged Illy as well.

Then, for a few minutes, the three friends were all hugging one another and pretending not to be crying. And then for some reason Pippa had also thrown herself into the group hug.

Legacy shifted from one foot to the next.

"This is—ah—all very nice," she said. "But we only have a few days to train. I was hoping we could get started tonight. At least see the courts?"

Horzst stepped away from the group hug. "Right," he said, pulling on a leather stocking cap. "You three ready?"

Pippa looked nervous. "Ready for what?" she said.

"Ready for the darkness," Horzst said.

"I mean, it's dark," Pippa said. "But I'm adjusting—"

"No, I mean the *real* darkness," Horzst said. Then he pushed open an earthen door in the floor.

"The deepest darkness," Illy said. Then he jumped in, followed by Horzst. Javi went next, and then Pippa made a little terrified squeak and stepped in behind him. Legacy closed her eyes. She imagined herself falling asleep in the old cycapress bower back home: the evening air cool, the fireflies lighting overhead. Then she stepped down into the darkness.

CHAPTER TEN

BELOW-BELOWGROUND

Legacy landed on a soft pile of dust and sneezed several times before standing up. When she stood and looked around, it really seemed like she had woken in the cycapress bower. In all directions, little spots of light were bobbing and weaving and bouncing, just like the fireflies back home.

"What *is* that?" she said, not sure who was around her.

"One of these!" It was Illy—or Horzst. And while she couldn't see him, she could see the bright white ball of light zooming toward her face.

She stuck her hands up and caught it just before it bounced off her nose. It was a tennis ball. Its fuzzy exterior glowed.

"Special stuff," Horzst said. He was holding one of the glowing balls up next to his face so she could see him. "Won't ever go out. They scrape it off the walls down in the wet mines."

Beyond him, shadowy figures were flitting back and forth on tennis courts with glowing white lines, striking glowing balls.

Legacy stared. "What—what *is* this place?"

Horzst peered at her. "You really don't know? You—I mean

she—paid for it. These are our new below-level courts. Courtesy of Silla and, ah—well, courtesy of that other Legacy."

"Part of her provincial initiatives?" Legacy said.

"Yep," Horzst said. "Build a few courts, keep people happy—even though their workdays are longer, and they have to mine deeper. Amazing what a few hours of tennis will do for the old mindset, even if you can't swim in the lake anymore, and you're inhaling metium fumes that will cut your life expectancy in half."

Now Illy stepped out of the darkness, leading another shadowy form, someone Legacy recognized. There were the extraordinarily broad shoulders, the legs so long her burlap jumpsuit fell short of her ankles, the sharp face, the close-cropped hair that glowed silver—

"Jenni! Hello!" Legacy grinned. It was surprisingly great to see her old competitor.

Jenni looked just as she had back at the trials: in the weak light from a glowing ball—strapped to a headband over her forehead—Legacy could see the same stubborn, uncompromising expression she'd seen when Jenni had challenged her to win the nationals on behalf of provis everywhere.

Legacy couldn't stop grinning. "It's great to see you!" she said. "This is Pippa, and this is Javi. They're my coaches, and—"

Something in Jenni's face made Legacy fall silent.

"How nice of you to come visit," she said, her voice cold as a hunk of prosite. "How *kind* of you to take the time to come visit us provis down in the mines."

Legacy grit her teeth. *That* Legacy, again, ruining everything.

"We've seen you in the news," Jenni was saying. "You've been talking about the provinces, but it sure doesn't sound like you know anything about them."

"No, no. There's been some confusion," Legacy said. "There's this . . . this *other* Legacy, and it's she who's—"

Javi stepped forward. "Jenni," he said, cutting Legacy off. "Listen. Legacy told us how skilled you are. She said you're the best opponent she's had in the republic. And we know that you are just as keen as we are to beat Silla and Gia." Javi paused, waiting for Jenni to agree. Jenni crossed her arms over her chest. Now Javi seemed intimidated. He looked around, lost, until Pippa stepped forward.

"What my friend here is trying to say," she said, "is that we hoped you'd train with Legacy. Spar with her, you know, in the darkness. Help her get ready to beat Gia at the Capari Open. Maybe you two could start with a few—"

"Nope."

They all turned to Jenni. Even Horzst and Illy seemed surprised. No one spoke for a moment, and they could all hear the distant bouncing of tennis balls on the surrounding courts.

"Busy," Jenni said. "Already training some promising kids here." And with that, abruptly, she turned to go.

Legacy lunged after her and caught her by the shoulder, but she wasn't prepared for the expression of fury on Jenni's face when she turned around.

"I have mouths to feed, just like you do," Jenni said, staring right into Legacy's eyes. "And it's getting worse. All this talk of these new mines? So far, all we've seen is a lot of hungry people, hungry kids, coming from all over for all these 'new jobs.' There's not enough food to go around. And the work is dangerous. People come down here and play tennis and take their mind off what's going on. But they're hungry and they're scared, and they're losing hope."

"I know," Legacy said, "I know, that's why I need your help—"

Jenni narrowed her eyes. "If you want my help, you can pay for it."

"Of course," Legacy said. "We're happy to pay. You name the price."

For a moment, Jenni seemed not to know what to say. Then she simply turned and marched away. Before she was lost completely in the darkness, she shouted back at them: "Tomorrow morning, then. Here. Seven a.m."

———

It was oddly cozy back in Illy and Horzst's house, and after they'd all shared some porridge cooked over the firepit—dinner, they called it, though Legacy thought it must be close to midnight—the friends sat around the glowing embers and caught up on the years that had passed since Javi had lived here.

"We were all a bunch of muscleheads," Javi said. "Did nothing but work our shift in the mines and come back here and lift weights."

Horzst grinned. "All three of us had plans to go to the academy. Make it big in the city."

Illy stroked his patchy beard. "But when the scouts came looking for builders, they only took Javi. I was too old, I guess, and you know about Horzst's ankle. And since then, shifts in the mines have gotten longer and longer. Silla's been ramping up metium mining since she came to power. And it's only gotten more intense lately. People speculate that something about Legacy Petrin"—he glanced at Legacy, and his face flushed with embarrassment—"I mean, something about you winning nationals caused her to want more metium in circulation. But regardless, shifts have gotten longer. You can't protest if you want to keep your job. Kids are coming here from all over the provinces, looking for jobs as a result of Silla's 'outreach.' Now you can't afford to say no to working longer hours, or going deeper."

Horzst nodded. "There have been a few benefits. The underground courts, for instance. But for the most part, the work's just gotten harder and the hours have just gotten longer."

Illy took off his leather cap and shook a little red dust into the fire. The embers sizzled and spat, and Illy returned the cap to his head.

"Now we barely have any time to life weights. Barely have time for anything, other than working."

Javi grinned. "I bet there's time for the occasional pepperfish feast," he said.

Horzst shook his head. "Not since the tunnels were dug under the lake. Now the lake's so polluted that you can't eat the pepperfish. Most of them are dead, and the ones that are left have two tails, or—"

Illy cut him off. "Stuff it, Horzst. You're scaring our guests, just before bedtime."

Even so, Legacy caught the heartbroken expression on Javi's face. She moved a little closer to him, and remained there while Horzst pulled the darts out of the third pallet and laid it down by the glowing embers. Pippa and Legacy piled in. Javi slept on the floor by their feet.

"Good to have you back, Javi," Horzst said before climbing into his cot.

Before she drifted off to sleep, Legacy thought of her father, back at the orphanage. She thought of the shapes in Villy's snow. If those shapes had terrified her so much, what would she make of the shapes in Gia's darkness?

And then she thought: *Only ten more days until Capari.*

———

Legacy woke to Javi shaking her shoulder. It was pitch-dark. "What time is it?" she mumbled. In the constant underground darkness, she was losing track of the hours.

"It's almost time to meet Jenni."

He handed her one of his homemade energy bars and prodded her toward the hole in the floor. Pippa and Javi jumped in behind her.

Belowground—or below-belowground—Legacy found that her eyes had adjusted to the constant darkness. Now she could make out enough of her surroundings to avoid constantly bumping her toes on the rocks and ridges jutting out of the rough-hewn corridors. She could see that the dust she'd fallen into was silver: prosite dust, not metium. And she could make out the forms of the tennis courts glowing in the distance.

Along with Pippa and Javi, both of whom were too tired to summon friendly conversation, she waited on the bleachers that had been cut into stone until finally—at seven fifteen—Jenni arrived with a bag full of the glowing balls.

Without saying a word, she dumped them all out at Legacy's feet so that they rolled in every direction.

"Gather a couple of those," she said, "and follow me."

Legacy bit her lip and got on her knees to start gathering the balls. Before she even grabbed one, Jenni was off.

"Hey—wait!"

Jenni didn't wait.

Legacy scrambled to her feet and jogged in Jenni's direction, heading downhill and leaving Pippa and Javi back with the glowing balls—and only source of light.

Soon she was engulfed in total darkness. The glowing lines of the tennis courts had faded behind them, and now even her adjusted eyes were of no help. This was a darkness so complete she felt like she was part of it. She felt like she wasn't even moving at all, like she was somehow treading water. Treading darkness.

She felt dizzy. If she reached out with her arms, she could touch the cold, damp stone of the walls. But if she reached up with her racket, there seemed to be no ceiling, only the endlessly downward-sloping ground under her feet.

Following Jenni, she headed deeper and deeper into the ground. The darkness was so thick she seemed to breathe it in. She found herself gasping for air. She reached out and grasped into the darkness, hoping to find Jenni, and for a moment she felt a rush of hope when she saw the outline of a form.

Except then the form turned to face her, and it wasn't Jenni.

It was—it was Gia.

Stunned, Legacy staggered back, tripped on a jutting rock, and fell flat on her back. Now, above her, there were three Gias, all in a row. They lined up, looking down at her. Then, in unison, they opened their mouths and started to laugh.

"Go back to where you came from, provi," one Gia said.

"We play real tennis here," said the second.

"We play for keeps," said the third, and all three started laughing.

"*Legacy!*" Jenni was standing over her, hands on her hips, holding out a glowing ball and a headband. "Pay attention! This is the court where we'll be training today—a little deeper now, a little darker. A little closer to the concentrated minerals."

Legacy swallowed. This was no time to be fearful. Reaching out, she took the glowing ball Jenni had offered, fastened it to her forehead using the headband, and looked around. Gia had disappeared, and what she saw was a single court, its lines unilluminated, merely shadowy streaks of white paint in the darkness.

"This court Silla doesn't know about," Jenni said. "It's where I train my best kids. Kids whose parents got lost in the tunnels. Kids who will go to work themselves by the time they turn ten or eleven. I still train them. I want them to know their own strength. Get them all accustomed to the darkest possible darkness."

Legacy hesitated. "We're really deep, aren't we?" she said.

"Pretty deep," Jenni answered.

"But what about the metium fumes?" Legacy said.

"What's with all the questions?" Jenni answered. "You're the one who wanted me to train you to play in the darkness."

"You're right," Legacy said, then headed out to the baseline.

They started with forehand drives: Legacy's least favorite shot, made harder now that she could barely make out her opponent. The ball seemed to emerge out of nowhere, surprising her so that she always seemed to be late, taking the ball as it was falling off the top of the bounce so that her spin was off and the balls flew long.

After her third shot flew out, Jenni yelled over the net. "Are you sure you're really Legacy Petrin?" she called. "The same Legacy Petrin who won nationals just a month ago?"

Legacy gritted her teeth. She tried to remember all the advice Javi and Pippa had given her in the forest. There was the stuff about meditating, and reps and sweat, and meditating in motion and—

"I have eight-year-old kids who can deal with the darkness better than this!" Jenni called. "If this is how you deal with some low-level-mine stuff, how are you going to manage against Gia's darkness in Capari?"

Legacy tried to blow on her fingers to calm her nerves. But her shoulders felt heavy. That weight was pressing on her again, and the net seemed to be growing. Jenni's voice seemed to be receding farther and farther into the darkness.

"Again?!" Jenni's voice echoed as another one of Legacy's returns arced long.

The weight felt heavier on Legacy's shoulders. She wasn't playing well. She was far from finding her groove, and even farther from summoning grana.

"Where's that famous light grana?" Jenni called. "Bet that would help you see in this darkness!"

Then another ball was pummeling toward her from the darkness on the other side of the net, which was growing taller.

It was a trick, Legacy knew. But in the darkness, she couldn't see where the next shot was coming from. She didn't have time to set up her feet, let alone calculate how much lower the real net was before—

THWACK. *Ugh*. The ball arced long.

"*Again?!*" Jenni's voice came from the other side of the net. "That's it. We're done here."

"One more try!" Legacy shouted over the net.

Silence. A pause. And then from out of the darkness a glowing ball shot straight toward her face.

Surprised, Legacy stumbled backward. Her head hit a wall, and the ball she'd been wearing bounced away, and she was suddenly engulfed in total darkness again. Legacy opened her mouth to shout for Jenni—or Pippa or Javi or really anybody—but before she could make a sound, she heard familiar, cold laughter.

Looming before her stood the three Gias. They pointed at her and laughed, until a rush of damp, metallic wind whooshed across Legacy's face.

It came from a huge green tennis racket that swept away the three Gias, all of them fading into wisps of green mist. From behind the racket, her father emerged. Now he leaned over her, coughing horribly. His whole thin frame was racked by each cough. And when he finally caught his breath, he looked Legacy in the eye and said: "You left me."

Legacy tried to murmur a response, but he cut her off. "You left me for this."

Then he shook his head and turned his back, but as soon as Legacy reached for him, he faded into green mist.

Legacy felt tears prick her eyes. This was some kind of trick of the darkness. A horrible trick. She had to get out of here. She rose to her feet and began to scramble forward, hoping it was in the direction of Jenni. All around her, as she lurched forward, using her hands on the walls to guide herself, she could see faces of strangers.

Strangers dressed like they did back home in Cora. They were cheering—but not for her. She knew who they were cheering for. They were cheering for *her*. For the other Legacy Petrin. The one they loved. The one they believed was a leader.

Legacy felt a cold void in front of her and stopped moving. She reached down and couldn't feel any bottom. Behind her were the cheering crowds and the Gias and her sick father. She turned and faced forward. Then she wiped the tears from her eyes and stumbled. She stumbled until she stubbed her toe on the net post, reeled back, and bumped into—Jenni.

"That's it," Jenni said, helping her up. "That's enough for this morning."

"Wait—Jenni. Those things I saw: Gia, my father. Did you see them, too?"

Jenni laughed but without any pleasure. "You have a long way to go, Petrin. A long way to go before you learn the first thing about darkness."

CHAPTER ELEVEN

A LIGHTNING STRIKE

Legacy pulled herself up through the hole in the floor and immediately winced at how bright the dim interior of the house was. After the darkness of the lower court, even Horzst's and Illy's candles were painfully bright.

Javi sat up from one of the improvised bench presses and grinned. "How'd it go, champ?"

Legacy grimaced. "Not well," she said. "Actually, it was a disaster. I've been sent home to rest. We came all this way to Minori to train, and—"

"What happened?" Pippa said. She was sitting cross-legged on the floor in front of a giant silver hunk of rock, which she appeared to be grating with a large, jagged cheese grater.

"I— The net started growing again. And I was hitting everything long. And then I got startled, and my head hit a wall, and I started seeing the strangest shapes in the darkness."

Pippa was nodding. "You're pushing yourself too hard," she said. "We walked miles yesterday, you were awake well past midnight, you didn't get a break—"

Javi jumped in. "Not this again! We didn't leave the orphanage and come all this way to have a day of rest."

Legacy thought of her father, coughing in bed. She thought of Hugo and Ink, taking care of the other littles. She thought of Capari, and False Legacy, and those shapes in the snow, and how well she'd have to play if she wanted to beat players like Villy.

"It's true," Legacy said, trying not to meet Pippa's eyes. "We came here so I could learn how to play in the darkness. I'll do better this afternoon. I promise."

———————

After lunch, down on the lower court, Legacy and Jenni returned to the same drill: forehand drives down the alley line.

This time, Legacy was ready. But Jenni was playing stronger. Her shots, which emerged out of the darkness only at the last second, were pummeling Legacy. Her first return she got late; the next she got even later, framing it and shanking it off to the side. In the darkness, she heard Jenni laugh. Determined, she told herself she'd prepare even before she saw the ball, and that worked for a few shots; after all, at least she knew the ball would come to her forehand. But even if she set up before she saw the ball, the waiting set her nerves on edge, and by the time the ball finally came, she practically fell on it.

Maybe, she said to herself, if her grana had been stronger, she could have seen better. But it was impossible to get her grana going when she wasn't returning shots. When her balance and her rhythm were off.

Lost in these thoughts, she didn't prepare in time for Jenni's next shot, and again she caught it on the frame, shanking it off into the darkness.

"Really, Petrin?" Jenni called from somewhere in the darkness. "Aren't you supposed to be a champion?"

Legacy closed her eyes. She thought of what Pippa had said in their meditation practice in the attic: *Just breathe*. She took a ragged, frustrated breath. Then she heard Pippa: *No, really breathe*. She breathed in so that her belly expanded like a balloon. She breathed out so that her belly button drew toward her spine. She breathed all of her frustration out into the darkness, and in its place, a quiet space opened up inside her.

There, she was in the forest. There was the softness of moss underfoot. The sound of whipwings flitting through the branches.

When she opened her eyes, she was still on the old court in the forest. Even in the darkness, she knew that court like the back of her hand. She knew exactly how many steps it took to get to the net. She knew exactly how far she'd have to lunge to reach the alley.

Jenni's shots started coming again, and this time Legacy caught them at the center of her strings. She prepared before she saw the ball. She set her feet. She set up her backswing. And as soon as she caught sight of the ball, she swung through with all her might, and her returns were heading straight and clean down the alley.

"Okay," Jenni said. "That's a little better, at least. Let's switch things up. Backhand cross-courts?"

Legacy smiled to herself. This was her favorite drill. This one she knew as well as she knew the motions of stirring the porridge.

Stirring the porridge! Suddenly Legacy felt it in her shoulders. She felt it in her hips. She felt her mind coming back down from the sky, settling once again into her body as she stirred the dirt in the corn porridge cauldron.

Then she remembered ghosting. Ghosting with a blindfold on. And finally, she remembered returning Gus's shots while blindfolded.

She didn't need to see. She didn't even need to open her eyes.

She *knew* this game. She *had* this drill.

On the baseline, Legacy let a ball bounce. Then she closed her eyes. She let it bounce again. She heard it thud against the ground, then ricochet back toward her hand. She felt its fuzz in her palm.

Then she took a deep breath, bounced the ball again, and hit a backhand cross-court.

The impact was perfect. She'd hit the ball right in the sweet spot. She felt that perfect twang shimmy out through her forearm.

She kept her eyes closed when she recovered the T, crouched low, waited for Jenni's return. She listened for the sound of Jenni's footsteps. She listened for the sound of Jenni's return. She knew just where it would bounce, and she was already there. She knew just how high the ball would rise, and when it reached its peak, she had already hit it.

The next sounds she heard were Jenni's footsteps, a swing, and . . . a miss.

Jenni had missed.

Legacy opened her eyes. She grinned. She'd hit a return too strong for Jenni to even make contact.

"That's it for the day," Jenni called from over the net.

"What?" Legacy said. "We just started!"

"Sure," Jenni said, stepping out of the darkness and approaching the net. "And now we're stopping."

Legacy stared. Her face felt hot. "Hey," she said. "That was a good shot."

Jenni was still moving off court.

"I mean, I understood before—I was playing terribly. But that was a good shot. I think I'm starting to get a handle on how to play in this darkness—"

Jenni laughed harshly. "Then you don't need me anymore," she said. "And I certainly wouldn't want to waste any of your hard-earned blood money."

"Listen, Jenni," Legacy said, stepping into the tunnel and blocking Jenni from leaving. "I know you don't like me. I don't need you to like me right now. I just need your help getting better at this."

"But do you, really?" Jenni said, pushing past her and heading up the long incline to the upper courts. "You have thousands of fans. Anywhere you go in this country, you'll be able to get people to do your bidding. And in that case, why come here? Why train with *me*?"

Legacy frowned. "You can't punish me just because people like me."

Jenni grinned over her shoulder and kept moving toward Illy and Horzst's house. "You think people *like* you? They don't like you—they're afraid of you! They know you're Silla's stooge. And they know what Silla can do to an unknown person from the provinces."

Legacy groaned. "That's not me. I know you don't believe me, but I don't know how else to say it. That person who's supporting Silla's job initiatives: that's not me!"

Jenni didn't stop moving.

Legacy ran to catch up. "I'm telling you," she said. "That Legacy—she's not me. I'm not like her. I would never do Silla's bidding. I would never—"

But Jenni was already pushing the door up into Illy and Horzst's house and climbing through it. When Legacy followed her, Jenni was waiting with an expression of unadulterated annoyance.

"Okay, Petrin," she said. "Sure. We all have our different selves. I'm glad you're so in touch with that."

"No, you don't understand," Legacy said. "That's not me at all—"

"It's actually not her," Pippa chimed in from her place on the floor, where she was still grating her enormous silver rock.

Jenni gave her a cutting look. Then she turned back to Legacy. "It's *wonderful* that you're embarking on this process of self-discovery," Jenni said. "But just so you know: while you explore the different sides of yourself, people down here are dying. We've always worked hard, and we've always known darkness. But these new metium mines that you and Silla are digging? The ones that go down under the lake, down where the lava's still flowing? Well. *That* special new suffering is completely on you. And the sad thing is, you'll never know it. You'll go your whole life completely insulated from the effects of the policies you've supported. You'll never understand the kind of suffering you've inflicted. You'll never understand, and you don't even care."

Legacy felt her frustration rising. In the city, they made assumptions about her because she was from the provinces. Now Jenni was making assumptions about her because she'd spent time in the city. Maybe she didn't understand everything about Silla's plans, but she did care. Everything Legacy had done since she first left the orphanage and went to the city was because she cared, either about the littles or Van or Pippa or Javi. Because she cared about the provinces. And for that very reason, she was now being told that she was an outsider, that she could never understand anyone from the provinces.

"You act as though I've never lived in the provinces," Legacy said. "As though I've never known anything—"

"You *haven't*," Jenni said. "Not anything like this."

Legacy stepped forward. "Then take me," she said. "It's not me, I'm not supporting those tunnels, but take me down there. I want to see them."

Pippa stood. "Me too," she said. "I'm coming with you."

Legacy shook her head. "You don't have to—"

"We want to," Pippa said.

"We all do," Javi said.

Jenni stared at them. "The fumes," she said. "They're dangerous. Especially if you're not used to them—"

"Take us down there," Legacy said. "We want to see them."

Legacy could feel herself being studied and appraised. Jenni seemed ready to either throw a tennis ball at her face—or hug her.

Instead, she shrugged. "Fine," she said. "But you better be ready for darkness. It's darker than the lower courts there. So dark it can swallow you up." Then she paused and gave Legacy one last look of appraisal. "But you know what? If you can handle that darkness, and those conditions? Well. Then you'll be ready for whatever Gia has in her."

———————————

The tunnel down to the new, deeper mines was better lit: one of Silla's improvements, no doubt. It had bright white torches on both walls and sloped steeply downward. It cut back—and cut back again, and again, and pretty soon Legacy lost count of how many turns they made, or how long they'd been descending. At some point, Legacy began to be able to smell the water that trickled down from the lake and through the walls. After a few more zigzags, she began to hear the water sizzle and steam. The walls were hotter now, and the air felt humid and thick.

They finally reached the bottom of the zigzagging path, and Jenni led them out into a vast, rust-red cavern that stretched beyond their vision. Legacy's mouth dropped.

"What *is* this place?" Pippa said.

"This isn't a mine," Javi said numbly.

"It is, though. It's the new Minori. Thanks to you."

All around them, people were rushing around, jumping, running, crouching, and hammering away at the sides of big trenches. Some of the miners were carting away crumbled red stone, and some were dusting off slivers of sparkling ore. That had to be the pure metium that Silla was so eager to mine. It was mesmerizingly beautiful in its raw form.

But everything else about this was ugly. The water slicked down the walls in red slurries, so people were slipping as they tried to haul away rock. The sounds of coughs ricocheted off the stone; some people were moaning even as they continued to work.

And there were kids down here. Kids not much older than Hugo and Ink. And people far too old to be working in these conditions. Legacy watched as one stone-laden cart rolled over the foot of a miner, who leaped backward in pain and fell to the ground. No one went to help him.

Legacy was about to rush over, but Jenni held her firm. "Strict rules down here, Petrin. Strict rules. You don't want to get on the wrong side of the shift manager."

Legacy stared. She wasn't even holding her racket, but her fingers were tingling. The roots of her hair were hot. The old man was still on the ground, writhing in pain. Others were moving around him, their shoulders stooped.

Her father's stoop had grown worse in the days before she'd left for the city, when his worries about the orphanage finances had started to weigh on him more heavily. With her face starting to burn, Legacy wondered—not for the first time—what would have happened to him if she hadn't been able to win money and bring it back from the city. What if the orphanage had closed? What if all the littles had ended up here in the mines? What if her father had been forced to find work here, and what if that were him—

The whole cavern lit up like in a lightning strike.

Legacy smiled in satisfaction. Finally. Her grana: it was back. Only now it was getting stronger and stronger. It felt as though it were tearing her skin.

"Leg . . . Leg!" Pippa was shouting. She sounded strangely far away, like she was on the other side of a vast ocean.

Legacy tried to reach for her friend, but she couldn't see anymore: her grana was exploding out of her in white sheets that rippled and broke in the darkness.

"*Leg!*" Javi shouted from somewhere across the same ocean.

But Legacy couldn't stop. She couldn't stop thinking about that old man with the injured foot. She couldn't stop Silla's plans. She couldn't stop any of this.

She felt her feet cramp and gasped in pain. Then her calves suddenly clenched as well. She fell to her knees. A blazing field of grana expanded off her skin as her pain and anger swelled inside her. Then she heard a scream rising with the light that seared through the darkness.

CHAPTER TWELVE

A FISTFUL OF PEBBLES

Help her!" she heard someone shout from somewhere miles above her.

She looked up, tried to see Jenni. But she couldn't see her. Instead, she saw herself.

Herself?

Yes, it was her: the same brown skin, the same long curly hair, the same strong shoulders, the same burlap dress. Legacy Petrin, stepping confidently out of the darkness.

"Are you her?" Legacy asked. "Are you the other Legacy?"

The other Legacy laughed and smiled brightly. "What are you saying? There's no such thing as another Legacy!"

Legacy felt a thin sliver of relief slip through the darkness. "Okay . . . then who are you?"

The other Legacy laughed again. "*I* should be asking that! Who . . . are you?"

Legacy felt the thin sliver becoming a dagger. "I'm . . . I'm Legacy Petrin—"

"Are you?" A boy appeared in the darkness, standing beside her. He was smaller than her, and moved with a slight limp, and—

"*Van*," Legacy heard herself whisper. Her Van. The same Van with whom she'd run through the summer carnival, dressed as a dingbat. The same Van who always knew what she was going to say before she said it, before she even thought it.

False Legacy smiled brightly at Van. "What do you think?" she said. "Which one of us is the real Legacy?"

Van pushed his glasses up his nose. "I admit," he said, "the resemblance is truly extraordinary." Then he leaned forward and peered down at Legacy, who looked up at him from the floor. He was wearing a long silver scholar's robe, but otherwise he was just the same. There were his warm brown eyes, his skin the color of cycapress bark. He blinked and squinted at her through his glasses, and Legacy felt a surge of hope. This was it. All the confusion would be swept away. Van was her best friend: he'd be sure to recognize her.

But now he was shaking his head. "No, no," he said. "This one isn't right. She's quite imperfect. She doesn't have the same light."

False Legacy laughed.

Van laughed along with her.

The dagger pricked Legacy's chest.

Her eyelids closed. Her cheek was resting on cold stone. She realized she was passing out. Finally, she heard Jenni's voice, from somewhere very close by: "We have to get her out of here—now!"

The water was briny, and it went up her nose.

She shot upward, coughing and crying. A welter of voices all seemed to be expressing relief.

"What happened?" she asked. Blurry shapes were sharpening.

114

Candles, a kettle over some coal, what looked like a bench press. *Ah.*
Right. She was back at Illy and Horzst's house.

"You're safe," someone said.

"And you'll be fine."

"You just— There must have been some interaction between your
grana and the minerals in the mines. You started expressing, and you
weren't even holding your racket."

"No balance," someone said.

"Too strong for you to stand—"

Legacy blinked. It was Jenni's face hovering above hers. "Legacy,"
she said. "I'm sorry. I . . . I guess I thought you didn't care about what
was happening here."

Pippa had joined her. Now she shot Jenni a withering look. "Too
bad it took her nearly bursting into flames to prove to you that she's
really angry."

Javi's face joined Jenni's and Pippa's. "But hey, at least we can all
agree that was a pretty impressive demonstration of grana—"

Pippa was nodding. "Almost as strong as that other Legacy's—"

Jenni's eyes widened. "So it's really true? What you guys have been
saying about another Legacy?"

Javi nodded. "Now you're finally getting it. She's the one who's
been promoting the mines. She's the one who's sponsored by Silla."

"But she's a phony," Pippa said. "She's not really Legacy—"

Legacy sighed.

"I don't even know anymore," she said. "I saw her again, down
there in the mines. She was there, with Van—"

"Wait a second," Javi said. "What are you talking about? False Legacy was down there in the mines?"

Legacy shook her head. "I know it sounds made-up, but I saw her. I saw Gia, too, and my father, and Van. And Van: he didn't recognize me. He took one look at me and said that I wasn't really Legacy, and—"

Pippa was frowning. "Leg, False Legacy wasn't down there."

"Or Van," Javi said. "Or your father, or Gia."

Jenni blanched. "This, ah—this might be the metium talking."

Legacy, Pippa, and Javi all turned to stare at her.

Nervously Jenni shifted from one foot to the next. "It affects different people differently," she said. "Some people it makes fearful and obedient. Other people actually see their worst fears—"

Pippa was nodding. "It's the mineral associated with fear," she said. "I worried about how it might affect you, but I knew I couldn't talk you out of going down there. That's why I wanted to go with you. It's scary stuff. Balanced—the way we do in stringbinds—it spurs motivation, or causes players to be properly careful. But unbalanced, the way it is in those mines—"

Jenni hung her head. "I'm so sorry," she said. "I didn't know you weren't her. And I didn't know you'd see visions."

Legacy looked from her friends to the glowing embers under the kettle. In the shifting shapes of the fire, she almost feared she'd see them again.

"Visions," she repeated. "But they seemed so real. Van: he was just like himself. But different, too."

"Different?" Pippa said. She was wiping Legacy's forehead with a warm cloth.

"He'd changed," Legacy said. "It broke my heart. I guess I didn't realize how much I depended on the idea that somewhere, even far

116

away, my best friend was still thinking of me in the same way. Supporting me. Cheering me on. Even though I couldn't hear him."

"Maybe he still is!" Pippa said.

Legacy turned to her friend. "No, I don't think he is. Pippa. If you saw me, like this, like how I am, right now: scared of the dark and struggling to keep a single shot on the court. If you saw me like this, and you saw the other Legacy: glowing and tall and beloved by everyone in the country. If you saw both of us, which one would you like more? Which one would you want to be friends with?"

Pippa immediately began to answer, but Legacy stopped her.

"Don't try to comfort me," Legacy said. "Even you—I've heard you talking about how beautiful she is. How charismatic and inspiring that other Legacy must be."

Pippa hung her head. "You might be right," she mumbled. "Whoever she is—*what*ever she is—False Legacy has gifts. That much is true. She might be more poised and collected than you are. And she might smile more." Now Pippa looked up at Legacy. "But we're not friends because of your *gifts*. That's not why friends are friends. I'm friends with Javi, after all! And what gifts does he have?"

Javi mimed an arrow piercing his heart, then rolled his eyes.

Legacy shook her head and chuckled. "You two are impossible."

"Okay, I'm kidding," Pippa said. "And, Legacy, I'm sorry. I don't think I've been nearly as supportive as I could have been. As I *should* have been. I didn't realize how awful this whole False Legacy thing was. She's there all the time, isn't she? Lurking around in the back of your mind. Making you feel like you're falling short."

Legacy nodded.

117

Pippa looked down again. Then she reached to the rocky floor of Horzst and Illy's house and grabbed a fistful of the multicolored pebbles that were strewn everywhere in Minori.

"Here," she said. "Here's you."

She placed one of the rocks—gray, dull, basically unimpressive—in Legacy's hand. Legacy raised an eyebrow and was about to thank her friend for the odd gift, but Pippa spoke again. "And here's fake Legacy." She held up an identical-looking rock. If anything, it was slightly smoother, slightly shinier. It glittered in the candlelight. It had a faint sheen of purple.

"Beautiful, right?" Pippa said. "These two rocks, yours and mine, they're pretty much the same, right? Maybe this one's a bit shinier? But I get the sense this one doesn't have your hard head. Or your experience. Because that's what made you: the experiences you've had. The mornings you've spent looking after the littles. This visit to the worst part of the mines. The courage you showed running off to the city. Without those experiences, what are you?"

Pippa clenched her hand hard around the pebble she was holding. Then she opened her hand. In her palm was a crumbly pile of purplish dust.

"Dominu dust," Pippa said. "Very pretty. Very shimmery. And extraordinarily weak."

Legacy closed her own hand and felt the hard stone in her palm. When she opened her fist, the pebble remained.

"Yours is hard," Pippa said. "It's a compound, but it looks to be mostly prosite. Prosite: the mineral associated with process. The drills you do on court, the experiences you gain. It's tough as nails. And every prosite rock is unique, its shape determined by the process of its composition. That's what makes it unique. That's what makes it superior to prettier pebbles."

Legacy leaned forward and hugged her friend. "Thank you, Pippa. I love you. And—I'm sorry that I've been so impatient recently. It's been a really hard time."

Pippa grinned. "No explanations necessary," she said.

Javi had started to whistle. He was always uncomfortable with anything involving emotions.

Now he was muttering to himself. "Reps and sweat, sweat and reps, always important to keep up with one's training!"

Legacy laughed. "You're right," she said. "We came here to face the darkness, and that's just what we did. Now let's get home. Back to the court in the forest; back to our training."

Javi's face lit up. "That's what I'm talking about!" he said.

Pippa held up a velvet bag full of her prosite shavings. "I've got enough of this to add a little more to your stringbind," she said. "It'll connect you to your process."

"Reps and sweat," Javi said, warming to the direction of the conversation.

Pippa rolled her eyes. "Sure. And it'll also balance out whatever metium poisoning she's suffered here in the mines."

"Why wait any longer?" Javi said. "We're already wasting time we could spend on training."

"We'll leave first thing in the morning," Pippa said. She turned to Legacy. "I'll be happy to be back with my books—I've got some research to do that I think might help you if you face False Legacy at Capari."

"And I'll come with you," Jenni said.

The three friends turned to her in surprise.

Jenni shrugged. "You'll need a training partner, won't you? And I've got a bone to pick with that phony Legacy."

Before they left, Javi and Horzst and Illy shared another tearful group hug. Once again, Pippa joined in.

As a going-away present, Horzst and Illy gave them all leather caps and a bouquet of purple stalactites that Illy had cultivated on the ceiling.

"I'll be in touch," Javi said.

"So will I," Pippa said, to Horzst's and Illy's confusion.

"You guys are family," Javi said. "I won't ever forget you."

"Enough," Jenni said, shouldering her pack and heading for the door. "If Legacy's going to compete at Capari, we've got work to do and not much time to do it."

CHAPTER THIRTEEN

THE WIND IN
THE CYCAPRESS TREES

The bedsheet disguises Pippa had sewn were enough to win them a cart ride to Cora; from where they were dropped, it was only a few hours' walk to the orphanage, and while they climbed the road into the forest, Legacy smelled the cycapress and listened for the evening call of the whipwings and smiled. They'd been gone only a few days, but she'd missed the orphanage. She missed the sound of the littles' laughter, the chaos that followed in Zaza's wake, Ink's plays, Hugo's cooking, the general boisterousness that reigned in a houseful of children.

When they let themselves into the front gate, however, there actually wasn't much chaos. There wasn't much of anything. It was totally silent.

Only one whipwing was calling from the far side, but they couldn't hear any sounds of playing at all.

Where were the littles? What were they doing?

Legacy picked up her pace as she made her way up the long drive. Pippa and Javi took Jenni to go check on Gus, so Legacy was alone when she ran into the littles. A few were sitting together on the lip of the old well.

"Hey! Hey—you guys, you're not supposed to be sitting up on the well. You know that. What if one of you falls in and . . . What's wrong with you guys?"

The few littles on the well wall climbed down and sat silently with their peers in the grass. No one spoke.

"So you all missed me a lot, huh?" Legacy shook her head with an exaggerated look of hurt on her face.

"Hi, Leggy," Ink said. As soon as she spoke, all the other littles jumped to their feet and started running toward the front door. Ink hesitated, glanced once over her shoulder, then followed behind them.

Legacy called after them, but they weren't listening. She watched as they all filed into the main hall. Even Zaza held her place in line and sat at the main table in obedient silence.

Legacy stared at them. They looked . . . scared.

"What's going on, guys?" Legacy said.

They stared down at their hands.

Legacy felt a pit opening in her stomach. For a moment, she watched them, hands on her hips. Then she headed up the stairs to her father's room.

What was going on? Something must have happened. Did someone get hurt?

When she knocked on her father's door, he didn't immediately answer. The pit in her stomach was widening, reminding her of the pits she'd seen in Minori. Should she wait for him to answer? What if something was wrong? Legacy pushed open the door.

Her father was asleep, curled on top of the bed. He looked so . . . small. He almost looked like a boy. Not like the big, strong man she'd always known as her father.

As Legacy approached the bed, he lifted his head.

"Papa," she said, "how have you been?"

Her father sighed. "You're back," he said. "So soon. I'd hoped we'd have a little more time to recover." Then he turned away and burrowed under the covers.

Legacy stared at him, stunned into silence. "What do you—what are you talking about? I've been gone a few days, just like I told you. I've— What *happened*?"

"Please, Legacy. Just let me sleep."

She backed up and out of the room, and she closed the door. She was numb.

"Legacy?! Legacy!"

Pippa was calling for her. She rushed out to the back garden. "I can't find Gus," Pippa panted. "The littles say they haven't seen him in a while. What's going on?"

Javi and Jenni were running around the side of the orphanage. Javi lifted up his hand and opened it. It took a moment for Legacy to realize what it was: a flyer from the False Legacy exhibition match they'd seen at the far border of the forestry province. But how did it end up here?

"I found it out by the tennis court," he said.

"And someone's been playing down there," Pippa chimed in. "The grass is all torn up. It can't have been Zaza, can it?"

Legacy shook her head. There was no way. Even the most mischievous littles had their limits. They knew the tennis court was out-of-bounds. And what about Gus? And what about her father?

Her head started to reel. She felt dizzy. This was supposed to be going so much better. She had gone through the darkness of Minori and come out unscathed. Now she was home—and everything was wrong. It was like she was living in some terrible alternative—

She felt a sudden rush of dizziness and had to balance herself on the stone wall of the orphanage. "She was here," she said.

Jenni looked down at the flyer in Javi's hands. She pointed at the image. "Her?"

"Oh no," Pippa breathed.

"She was here," Legacy said. "There's no other explanation. She must have come back, and—"

"Um, Leggy? I mean, Miss Petrin?" Hugo poked his head around the edge of the garden shed. He looked terrified—more than usual.

Miss Petrin? Legacy shook her head, then went to kneel before Hugo.

"Hugo," she said, "I need you to tell me what she . . . what I did over the past couple days. Don't ask me why. Just . . . remind me what I did, okay? Everything you can remember."

Hugo, to his credit, followed directions. Over the next several minutes, he explained in gruesome detail how Legacy had spent all day training down at the court. She'd driven Gus to exhaustion, hardly letting him sleep, much less eat anything at all. At a certain point, according to Hugo, the littles had seen enough. They'd tried to stand up for Gus, but Legacy had told them to mind their business. That Gus was a dumb animal, and that dumb animals craved work. That their purpose was to work as hard as they could until they simply couldn't work anymore.

After that, apparently, the littles revolted. Ink had come up with a plan as elaborate as one of her plays. She'd distracted "Miss Petrin" while Zaza got her hands on some of Javi's construction glue and covered Legacy's racket handle with it. That had a wonderfully predictable result, and Gus had enough time to fly off into the deep forest. After that, Legacy had turned tyrannical and ordered all the littles into their beds for a full day. They didn't have anything to eat except Javi's home-made energy bars. The littles could hear Legacy and her father yelling at each other in the main hall, and Legacy's father had gone into the woods to look for Gus. He was gone for two nights.

When he came back, he came back alone, and he came back very weak. He'd been in bed ever since.

"Oh, and you apparently want us to call you Miss Petrin from now on." With that, Hugo's eyes filled with tears, and he seemed not to know whether to reach for a hug or to flee back up to his bedroom.

"Hugo," Legacy said with a calm voice, stroking one lock of his silky black hair behind his ear. "Could you please do three things for me. Go to the kitchen, and open up every bag of cornmeal you find. Open every jar of nipperberry jam, get out every comb of wild honey, take the cream out from the cooling box. Empty the cupboards. Bake a corn cake, make nipperberry truffles, see if we have enough cycapress nuts to make a batch of honey-nut ice cream. Cook everything you can think of. We're going to have a feast."

Hugo seemed to be brightening up a bit. Legacy smiled, and straightened his crooked burlap shift. "That's the first thing," she said. "The second thing is: Tell the rest of the littles that . . . that I was ill for several days. That I'm very sorry for my behavior. That we'll find Gus, and they shouldn't be afraid. That's the second thing. And the last thing—the last thing is very important: Please never refer to me ever again as Miss Petrin. From now on I'm Leggy."

Hugo beamed at her. "Okay, Leggy," he said, then rushed into the kitchen.

Legacy followed him and continued on to her father's room. She hoped she had time enough to explain.

She knocked on the door. No answer. Once again, her father was asleep. The last few days with False Legacy must have really taken it out of him.

Legacy tiptoed to the bed and sat in his reading chair. The blankets rose and fell with his breath. On his bedside table, he'd left a book propped open. Now she picked it up—*A Seaside Ceramics Reader*.

He never stopped learning, Legacy thought. He was curious about everything. He'd been a builder first, back when he met her mother. Then he'd built an orphanage from the ground up and learned about gardening and forestry, and now seaside ceramics, apparently.

"Don't lose my place," he muttered, then rolled over in bed. "I lost my bookmark."

Legacy smiled. "Seaside ceramics, eh?"

Her father gave her a stern look. "Cups," he said. "Cups in Capari have two handles, on account of the fact that most people in Capari have two hands. It seems like a solid piece of wisdom to me. Why don't our mugs have two handles?"

Legacy smiled. This was the old dynamic, from back in the days before she'd defied him to go to the city: the old prompting to guess, to speculate, to wonder about the world.

"Maybe," she said, "because most cups are small enough that you don't need to carry them with both hands. Our big water jugs have two handles."

Legacy's father smiled weakly. "That seems correct to me," he said. "So what are they drinking up there in Capari, anyway? I—"

Abruptly, however, he stopped talking. He looked as if he'd remembered something urgent.

Then he rolled away from her. "Go away, please."

Legacy felt like a cold air blew through her, like late autumn wind that stole away the last leaves from the nipperberry trees.

"I have to explain something," Legacy said. "And you have to believe me. That wasn't me. It's Silla. Silla has created some kind of double me. Some kind of False Me. Silla seems to be using me—False Me—to gain support for an awful initiative in Minori, but I'm not going to let her get away with it. And you have to understand that the person who fought with you—the person who treated Gus cruelly, and punished the littles, and let you go off into the forest alone—that person wasn't me. And I don't know exactly what that person said, or did, but—"

Not for the first time, Legacy found herself apologizing for something she hadn't done. But this time was different. Her father was different. He looked smaller, and sicker: unlike the father she'd always known.

No words she could say could unravel the damage that had been done over the past several days. Now, finally, instead of trying to finish her explanation, Legacy stopped. Tears brimmed in her eyes. She buried her face in her hands until she felt her father's hand on her arm.

His voice was gentler than usual. "Legacy," he said. "My girl. I've grown old. And they say that age and wisdom go together. Sometimes, though, I am very unwise. Sometimes I'm just a fool. I don't know anything about 'doubles,' or whatever it is that you're talking about. But I know that you're telling the truth. I can hear it in your voice. And I know that I was foolish to ever think you could have said the things you said. I'm sorry."

Legacy grasped his hands and leaned forward to kiss his cheek.

"Papa," she said, "how could you believe that girl was me? I could never be cruel like that, to you or Gus or the littles. You know that, right? You know I'm not a cruel person?"

Her father started to speak, then doubled over with a coughing fit. It was getting worse. His cough: Legacy had never heard it like this.

When he'd recovered himself, he smiled sadly. "What I was going to say," he said, "was that we all have the capacity to be all things. I mean, there are limits. I was never all that good at tennis. But, in our hearts I mean, we all can be all things. I've had my unkind, regrettable moments. And your mother—you should have seen her when the provincial surveyors came through before you were born, telling us they were going to lay down a road right through the middle of our raspberry patch. Right through the heart of the gardens. They were lying, of course. They just wanted us to bribe them to leave and take their crummy road elsewhere. I was ready to pay. Your mother wasn't. She had a rage that day like I've never seen. She was incandescent. She looked like a lit match. It seemed like the tips of her hair were on fire."

Legacy was laughing, in spite of herself. "I don't believe it," she said. "I always imagined Mom was so gentle—"

"She was! But she could also get angry. And when she had a good reason for anger, a righteous reason for anger, she could summon a strength that could have equaled the Great Fire. There were six or seven surveyors, all of them bigger and more powerful than your mother. But you know what? She scared those crooks away. They went running off down the driveway." Having slipped into that memory,

Legacy's father fell silent for a moment. He closed his eyes. His face was older, and more drawn than Legacy had ever seen it. And yet now he seemed to have returned to that time, and a smile hovered on his face.

Then he opened his eyes and smiled at his daughter. "If your mother could touch that kind of anger, it only shows that we all have all kinds of secret capacities. I know that. I know that you, like your mother, have the capacity for enormous anger. But I also know that, like your mother, your heart is full of love. And most of the time, you make the right choice. When anger is necessary, you choose that. But when love is possible, that's what you choose. When goodness is an option, that's what you choose. That's who you are. I know this because I've been your father all of your life. You are a person who chooses goodness."

Legacy smiled. She kissed her father again. Then, so he wouldn't see the tears in her eyes, she picked up the ceramics book. She began to read from a passage describing the specific kind of glaze that people in Capari use on their clay, mixed with specific ratios of sea salt and shell gleam, squid-ink black and barnacle brown.

It was extraordinarily boring, and soon her father was dozing off. Legacy watched him for a moment. Her father. The only parent she'd ever really known. Then she tiptoed out of the room.

Pippa was waiting for her in the hall, along with Jenni and Javi.

"We found it!" Javi said.

"*She* found it," Jenni said.

Pippa grinned and held up a green book with a red wax seal—the book, Legacy recalled, that she'd bought from the peddler who'd visited the orphanage before they left for Minori. "We still don't entirely know how it all works, but this book is a pretty good start!"

Legacy took a step closer. She brushed her finger over the cover: STRINGING FOR DOUBLES.

"It's over two hundred years old," Pippa was saying, "and it's written in archaic language. And fairly cryptic archaic language, at that. Even back then, in the ancient days, the practice was forbidden, so the book's basically written in code. But from what I can tell, the practice consisted of creating what was known as 'string children.' For some reason I haven't figured out yet, it seems not to have worked for adults. But kids: they had some quality that could be caught in the threads. So you could make a double of your best friend, if she'd just moved to a different part of the country. Or—and this is important—a double of your fiercest tennis opponent, so that you could practice against her."

"So they could play tennis!" Jenni said.

"And display grana," Pippa said.

"And perform on court even better than their actual double."

"They look just like real children," Pippa said, "and move just like real children, and talk just like real children. But they're woven out of threads. And they don't have free will. They—they have to obey the will of their creator."

Legacy stared. "And you think that other Legacy might be a string child?"

Jenni nodded energetically. "Created by Silla to do her bidding."

Legacy looked at her new friend and remembered what her father had just said: *That's who you are. You are a person who chooses goodness.*

"So she's like me," Legacy said, "but she can't make her own choices?"

Pippa flipped through her book and pointed at what was indeed a very long footnote. "That's what it seems to say here," she said. "Though to be honest, it's not entirely clear. Like I said, the whole book's written in code. Or just written by an extraordinarily terrible writer."

Legacy thought for a moment: if her father was right, if Pippa was right, what made her who she was, and made False Legacy false, was that Legacy could choose to be a good person.

Legacy closed her eyes. She could smell something wonderful happening in the kitchen. Hugo had gotten to work, apparently.

She smiled at her friends. Then she led them down to the main hall. The littles were waiting for them.

Now Legacy looked at their soft faces. Their curls, their chubby cheeks, their sweet little hands. They smiled back at her, a little nervously. She wondered how she could tell them that she wasn't her. That—in the wide world that they didn't yet understand—it was possible that someone with ill intentions might create a version of yourself with no will of her own: a perfectly lifelike automaton meant only to serve. She glanced at Ink, already too quiet. She thought about Hugo, already too fearful.

Then she cleared her throat. "As you heard from Hugo," she said, "I was a little out of sorts the past few days. I hope you all can forgive me for my bad behavior. All of us can be bad sometimes. Grown-ups, high consuls, national champions . . . everyone. The important thing is to apologize."

Zaza raised her hand. Legacy nodded at her.

"Is Gus coming back?"

Legacy forced herself to smile as though she were confident. "We're going to find Gus. That is a promise."

With that, most of the littles jumped up and began running to the kitchen to prepare themselves to hunt for Gus: big hunks of wild honey and corn cake, mostly for him, a little for them. Only Zaza stayed behind. She had another question for Legacy. One that she seemed more comfortable asking quietly.

She toddled over to Legacy, put one chubby brown hand on her knee, and leaned in to whisper in her ear. "Is your papa okay?" she said.

Then she looked up at her worriedly.

Legacy picked her up and carried her toward the barn. "Let's go see if we can find Gus," she said. And while she walked, she took a deep breath. Then she took another: a breath so big she could hear it. A breath so big she sounded like the wind in the cycapress trees.

Let him be there, she whispered, too quietly for Zaza to hear. She didn't know who she was saying it to, or who to thank when she and Zaza came to the barn and found the littles encircling Gus.

Legacy dropped to her knees. She pressed her face to his.

"Forgive me?" she whispered into his velvety muzzle.

Then she opened her eyes, and even if he was a pyrus, it was clear that he was smiling.

———————

Late that night, Legacy woke up Pippa and Javi. She had been staying up with her father. Reading to him from the book on Capari. She hadn't realized right away what had happened. It only seemed as though, once again, he'd returned to that other time. The time when it was the three of them. But then she knew that he was gone.

For a long time, Pippa and Javi hugged her, and Legacy cried. She hadn't cried like that in years. Maybe she hadn't cried like that ever. She had felt alone a lot in her life: when she was the only provi at the academy, when Van walked away down the long driveway, when she saw that everyone in the republic loved her double more than her, when she realized how much Jenni loathed her. But even then, even in the most intense moments of her loneliness, she'd known that she could return to her father. And now? Now who would she return to?

Pippa and Javi didn't try to comfort her. In their own way, they'd also lost families. They didn't try to make her feel better; they only held her until she'd cried herself out in the darkness.

Then, finally, before the sun rose, Legacy went out into the forest. She walked over the moss, under the low-hanging boughs of cycapress. And then she looked at the court her father had built with her mother.

Everything she did from now on: she'd do it for her father.

CHAPTER FOURTEEN

CHERISH WOOD, ONCE BENT

Over the next day, Pippa and Javi and Jenni took it upon themselves to perform the day-to-day duties of the orphanage. Hugo and Ink were both too devastated, too young, to stand up and take responsibility in such a raw moment. So Javi cooked, Jenni cleaned, Pippa washed pajamas and swept the pine needles that piled up in windblown heaps in the courtyard. They played with the littles and they scrubbed the walls. They kept the place alive, and as organized as possible.

Legacy had other things to do.

With her friends' help, she had carried her father's body to a little plot of scissor grass at the edge of the forest, up near where he and Legacy's mother had carved out a garden decades ago. A piece that had been totally unperturbed by the Great Fire. It was just a little clearing, ringed by tall silver grasses, but she and her father had often walked here when he had been healthy. It was the perfect spot to sit and rest after a long hike through the forest. And now it was where he would rest, forever.

She had found an old gardening spade that must have been Van's before he left for the city, and she dug with that. The land at the edge of the forest, on the side that had been restored after the fire, was soft and yielded easily, and soon she had finished. Her face and arms were covered in dirt and sweat, and tears rolled down her cheeks as she lowered her father into the ground. She was essentially an orphan now, too.

That thought kept running through her mind. It didn't make her any sadder than she was. It was just the way it was now. She took a spadeful of dirt and let it slip down into the grave. Then her body let go. At first it was the sheer exhaustion of having dug and dug under the summer sun that made her drop the spade and sit down on the pile of dirt she'd made. Then it was the feeling of regret that she'd been away for so long, training in the city and playing a game—a game—while her father had apparently gotten more and more unwell. She hadn't been there for that; she hadn't been there for him. She missed so many of the last months of his life. And there wouldn't be any more, ever again.

"You need help with . . . anything?" Javi asked, with uncharacteristic softness in his voice.

"We got all the littles to nap, or at least to pretend to nap. And we thought you might want some company," Pippa said.

Jenni—who hadn't ever known Legacy's father—seemed to wish she had something to say, but now, with unusual shyness, she hung back, as if unsure.

Legacy stood and turned and saw her friends, who had come all the way from the orphanage. She had barely talked to them all day. She had barely talked, period. She was so overwhelmed, so exhausted, that she still didn't know what to say.

Jenni cleared her throat. Pippa looked concerned. Javi stepped forward.

"Hey, well, I don't know how you Foresters do things, but Jenni and I wanted to tell you about how we used to pay our respects back in Minori." He held up a long and silvery stick. Its bark was almost perfectly smooth, and it shined in the sun. Legacy had never seen anything like it.

"Actually," Jenni said, "it's a lot easier here in Cora, because these cherish trees actually grow around here. They're rare, but they do grow here. Back in Mino, we had to pay some traveling merchant for a piece of cherish wood, and it was never this healthy-looking."

"Here, look," Javi said. He took the stick in both hands. It was very long and as thick as her racket handle. It looked like it could make a fearsome weapon, or a fishing pole. But Javi was able to bend it into an arc with ease. "Cherish wood, once bent, will always stay like this. It won't ever unbend; and it'll never break. What we do in mines is bend it so it's the height of someone close to the deceased."

Javi brought the cherish stick over to Legacy and bent it so it was just a little higher, from the bottom of the arch to the top, than Legacy. "Then we place it in the ground right by the resting place. May I?"

Legacy nodded.

Javi did, then pressed the ends into the earth so that the top of the arch was exactly as tall as Legacy. "I promise you it'll never bend, or break, or fall over, or budge. Not for anything. And now your father has this arch here, always beside him, and it's just exactly the size of the person who meant everything to him. A version of you will always be with him."

Legacy looked at the arch. It *was* beautiful. It looked so much like an arched doorway. She wished more than anything that she could step through and go back in time, if just to spend a little more time with her father.

"Thank you, Javi," she said. "Thank you, Jenni. It's perfect." Her voice was scratchy from not using it since the early morning.

Jenni smiled shyly. "Actually," she said, "there's one more thing." She reached down the base of the arch, where the silver wood was driven into the dirt. She took a pocketknife out of her shift and cut a small slit into one side of the base, and then another slit that joined the other, and loosened out from the wood a small silver wedge. She handed it to Legacy. "You take this piece. So, it'll be with you, too."

The four friends were quiet for a moment. They let the wind whisper through the tall grass. The somberness of the moment was broken only by a tiny sneeze that came from behind them, where the path from the forest entered into the clearing. They all turned to see Zaza at the head of a parade of very tired-looking littles, one of whom was sneezing with abandon.

"I think it's the grass," Zaza said sheepishly.

"Where's Hugo and Ink? I thought I told you all to stay put!" Javi said, irritated.

"We wanted to come and help . . . say goodbye," Zaza replied.

Javi, for once, just bit his lip. And Pippa rushed over and hugged Zaza. Then she picked her up and led the rest of the littles back to the grave, and they gathered around the new silvery arch. And they all said goodbye.

Legacy lingered while the others peeled off and returned to the orphanage. Dazed, she slowly lifted her head to the sky, where a breeze was sending waves and shimmers through the canopies of the cherish trees. The leaves, silver underneath and dark green on top, moved in unison, like a school of fish. Watching them, she felt hypnotized.

Then the leaves began to change. It was strange, and Legacy didn't look away, for fear that it would stop if she did. She didn't even blink. The leaves began to turn bright orange. Not like they did in the fall—but like the sunset over the olive trees.

Legacy's heart began to beat harder. She approached the base of a tree, all the while gazing upward. Blue—like the water in a northern river—spread out from the veins of the leaves.

Soon the whole canopy was the same color, and it was almost hard to see against the blue sky.

Then they began to change again, becoming silvery, like thousands of silvery butterflies settling on the cherish tree branches. Like leaves under the starlight.

In awe, Legacy watched until the last cherish leaf turned silver. There had been a lot of mysteries recently: growing courts, rising nets, shapes in the snow, faces in the darkness. Most of these mysteries were unsettling. But this one felt different. She didn't need to know what was happening to these leaves. And in one sense, she already understood. Like herself, the leaves were changing. They had to. Her father was gone now.

But the leaves weren't falling. They were just becoming something new.

———

Legacy felt numb that whole day. Only when the sun was setting beyond the olive groves, gilding them so that they looked like bronze statues, did she take Gus and her friends down to the court to practice. At first, Gus took it easy on her. The fireballs he spit over the net barely singed her racket. Still, there was something comforting in being back on court. They practiced the same drills she'd been practicing with Javi since he invented her new training regimen. Over and over again, she repeated the same motions: stirring the cauldron, then ghosting; ghosting blindfolded, then playing with the same blindfold.

It helped her return to her body: the roll of her foot from heel to toe, the transfer of her weight, the final flick of her forearm. As she played blindfolded, her mind was part of her body; they were one and the same. Her head was full of the sound of footsteps, so there wasn't room for thoughts about whether she could repeat her performance at the national championships. There were only footsteps, and the weight of her racket, and the feel of her grip, and the strings striking the ball. Nothing mattered except for the heat in her forearm when she struck a forehand, the faint burn in her thighs when she lunged for a drop shot. It was hard work, but, in a strange way, it was also easy: it was a return to herself, a return to what she was meant to be doing.

"Do you need a rest?" Pippa called from the sideline.

"Keep going, more reps!" Javi called.

And then suddenly Legacy knew the solution to their disagreement. She almost laughed in the fading light of the forest. It was so simple. "It's both," she called back to them, smiling. "It's drills and rest, meditation and reps. It's listening to my body."

Swinging her Tempest, she returned his fireballs, harder and harder, until Gus was glistening with sweat. Then Jenni stepped in. Legacy removed the blindfold. The sun had set: now they were playing in darkness.

Once again, as they had in the mines, Jenni's shots flew out of the darkness: as strong as Gus's fireballs, but with more variety and less predictable spin. It was nearly impossible for Legacy to see the ball until it was too late.

But Legacy didn't need to see the ball. She closed her eyes. She listened for the sound of it striking Jenni's strings. Then she waited. She knew this court. She knew the bounce of its surface. Then she moved forward and swung.

Ping. She felt it hit the center point of her racket.

The longer they played, the more certain she felt. She counted her footsteps. She felt the rhythm of the game in her body. As she lunged around the court, chasing down Jenni's shots, she felt something inside of herself returning.

She sent a backhand spinning across her body and back toward the far corner, way out of Jenni's reach. She opened her eyes. Jenni looked at her almost like she was offended.

Legacy smiled and shrugged. That was *joy* she felt rise in her chest.

That night, once the littles had been fed, Legacy strolled past the well through the garden. Her father used to take early-evening walks around the grounds. When she was young, she would follow behind, imagining him inviting her to join him. Imagining a different father than she had—or than she'd had since her mother left. One who was more lighthearted. Full of joy on days other than just the summer carnival.

Now she headed toward the steps into the kitchen. She wanted to go up to her father's room to start organizing his things. She wanted to keep all his trinkets, all his collections of odd objects: pebbles and leaves, blue wazoon feathers and butterfly wings. Even at his sternest moments, he'd always loved the forest. He'd come home from every walk with evidence of his love for it: a twig covered with silver-green lichen, a heart-shaped piece of petrified wood.

Since his death, she'd idly thought about transforming the old tool-shed into a kind of natural history museum, where she could display all his collections. Walking into the kitchen, she was thinking about possible arrangements for the museum when she heard Pippa's voice filtering down through an open window.

"If we had more time," Pippa was saying, "I'd agree with you. But the Capari Open is in eight days. Maybe we just tell her that she should sit this one out."

It was Javi who responded. "And let Gia and Silla and that False Legacy loser sweep into easy victory?"

"And give them more power?" Jenni said. "And let them ruin more provinces like they've ruined Minori?"

"Jenni," Pippa said, "I know what's going on in Minori was hard for you and . . ."

Legacy leaned into the orphanage wall. She was right under the window into the attic, the one Pippa had covered with rough cloth, so their voices were muffled.

"But she needs time to mourn," Pippa said.

Javi was silent. Then, finally, a murmur Legacy couldn't hear.

"Yes," Pippa said. "Yes, there's no getting around it."

Silence. Then—the curtains were thrust open, and Legacy ducked down. She didn't love eavesdropping on her friends, but, well, she'd already gone this far.

Pippa again: "Here's the plan. We skip Capari. Give her time. She needs to make sure she has her mind in a good place. No more of this lengthening court stuff. No more of this growing net. I'll work on some mantras—"

"And we'll keep working on my new drills."

"I'll get her ready for match play," Jenni said.

"Yes, *and together* we'll get her in shape for the next Open tournament after Capari. And we'll just have to hope that Silla and Smiley don't keep up their campaign in the mines, or start any new provincial outreach programs in the Forest of—"

Legacy couldn't stop herself. "Absolutely *not!*" she yelled up at the window. In no time, she saw Pippa's and Javi's and Jenni's faces peering out.

"Yes," she said, her face hot with embarrassment. "I was eavesdropping. And yes, I'm sorry. But no, I will not skip the Capari Open."

"Leg," Pippa said in her gentlest voice. "Leg, you just lost your father—"

Legacy held tightly to the piece of cherish wood in her fist. She could hear her father's voice. You choose goodness, he'd said.

She thought of that old man, deep in the deepest levels of the new mines in Minori. She thought of her father's love of the forest. She thought of the littles.

"I'm playing Capari," Legacy said. "I'm playing, and for that matter, I'm winning."

She could see Javi starting to grin. Pippa glanced at him uneasily.

"Let's do it," Javi said.

Pippa sighed.

Jenni grinned.

"We've got six more days to train," Legacy said. "Javi and Jenni, I'm going to need you to help me on court. And, Pippa? I just need you to figure out more of the details about how Silla made that other Legacy. Javi, it's like you've always said: you can't win if you don't know what you're competing against. Let's find out what her strengths are. What her weaknesses are. And how I'm going to beat her."

In the morning, when Legacy joined her friends for an early breakfast before heading out to the court, Pippa was detailing the logistics of Legacy's registration for Capari.

"Like I said," she was explaining, "the other Legacy is already registered as Legacy Petrin. So I took the only other approach I could think of, and registered Legacy for the qualifiers under an invented name."

Legacy took a bite of corn porridge. "What do you mean, the qualifiers?" she said. "I'm the national champion. That should guarantee me a seeded spot in the main draw and—"

"Yes," Pippa said, "but, for the time being, until it's the right moment to prove yourself, you're not Legacy Petrin."

Legacy sighed. "Right," she said. "I always forget."

"So who is she?" Jenni said. "What's her new name?"

Pippa flushed. "I, uh, I sort of panicked."

Jenni giggled.

Legacy glared. "And?"

"Pegacy Letrin," Pippa said. "Nickname Peg?"

CHAPTER FIFTEEN

DAWN BREAKS, LIGHT PLAYS

On their way out to the court for the morning training session, the friends fine-tuned their plan. They knew, of course, that if Legacy was going to play under the name Pegacy Letrin, she'd have to play in disguise at the beginning of the tournament. And she wouldn't remove the disguise until Legacy had earned a chance to prove herself in a match against False Legacy. What they hadn't decided was what that disguise should be.

"We'll be in the public eye," Pippa was saying. "A cap and some face paint won't do the trick."

"We'll have to look real," Javi said. "Real but unrecognizable. Like players from some part of the country that don't usually show up at the big prestigious tournaments."

"Minori," Jenni said.

"What?" Pippa said. "We're talking about people, not places—"

Jenni made a face. "We can dress like we're from Minori. Mineral dust, cropped hair, leather caps—"

Pippa's eyes widened. "It's perfect!" she said. "They'll never know. Leg won't mind cropping her hair, and—"

She paused. Legacy looked at her. "What?"

"Well, you know that you won't be able to show your grana, right?"

Legacy felt the corn porridge she'd eaten for breakfast hardening into a lump in her stomach.

Somehow—in all their talk of disguises—she hadn't thought that she'd also have to disguise her grana.

"That's how they know you," Pippa was saying.

"You know the saying," Javi said. "'No one shines brighter than . . .'"

"Legacy Petrin," Legacy said. "So I'll have to get through the tournament without using my grana. I'll have to beat all those other players from the academy, using whatever grana they have, without accessing mine."

"Right," Pippa said.

"Ugh," Jenni sighed. "As if training at the academy weren't advantage enough."

"It's unfair, I know," Pippa said. "But if the idea here is to prove that you're the real Legacy, you'll have to prove that you shine brighter than her. And to do that, you'll have to play her."

"And you won't get to play her," Javi said, "if they arrest you for impersonating her."

Legacy nodded. "So all I have to do is beat the best players in the republic—players like Villy Sal or even Gia—without using any grana. And if I can do that, I'll have to play a string child who—according to everyone in the country—has the strongest grana they've ever seen."

"It's a tall order, I know," Pippa said. "But you've been playing so well in practice, much better than you were when you were at the academy, and I'm still studying the old books to see if there are any tips to help you play your string child. I feel like there's something there—something important—even if I haven't quite grasped it."

"And in the meantime," Javi said, "you know what I always say—"

"Reps and sweat," Jenni said, rolling her eyes at Legacy, then ran out to take her side on the court Legacy's father had built in the forest.

After her morning training session, Legacy reported to the attic for a meditation session with Pippa. Before she sat down, however, Legacy glanced at the enormous green book on Pippa's table. "Have you learned anything new?" she said. "Any strengths or weaknesses of string children?"

"Meditation first," Pippa said, and set a candle between them. "Now breathe," she said.

And for a while, Legacy breathed. She breathed out all of her fears about competing without grana; and when she breathed in, she could hear the sound of the wind in the cycapress leaves.

"Now," Pippa said, "I want you to bring to mind a person you've recently had some conflict with. A misunderstanding. A failure of communication. Someone who's been bothering you when you're playing. Someone you can't get off your mind when you're trying to focus on tennis."

Legacy tried to imagine this. But she kept thinking about False Legacy: the strength of her light grana, those columns of brightness. How she seemed taller than Legacy herself. More cheerful, too. And more focused.

She opened her eyes. "Pip," she said. "Can we please just talk about False Legacy first?"

Pippa narrowed her eyes. "You've said you feel a weight pressing down on your shoulders. What we're trying to do here is lift some of that weight. Get you playing light again. Get you playing with a sense of freedom."

Legacy sighed and closed her eyes.

"A person," Pippa said, "who you miss, or someone you wish were by your side."

Which of the many people? Legacy thought. Her father, so recently gone? Her mother, whose absence had been a hole she'd nearly fallen into so many times throughout her childhood? Van, who was off in the city, studying economics?

Van. On the floor of her mind, her vision from the deepest mines reappeared: Van in his scholar's robe, standing beside False Legacy. Telling Legacy she was an impostor.

Van, whose face she'd imagined she'd seen in those pictures of False Legacy at Silla's charity event.

She felt a sharp pain in her side.

Pippa was talking in her soothing meditation voice.

"Now I want you to lie down on your back. And imagine that person in miniature. A very tiny version of that person, no bigger than a figurine. And that miniature person is sitting on your chest."

Legacy breathed. The pain eased. She lay down on the dusty floor of the attic. Then, with her eyes closed, she imagined tiny Van on her chest. In her mind's eye, she looked at tiny Van.

He was wearing his scholar's robe. He pushed his glasses up on his nose. "You're not as good as her," he said. "You're not as good as the other—"

Legacy sat up. She didn't want to see Van anymore. She didn't want to think about Van. She glanced at the green book on the table.

"Pippa!" she said. "Tell me what you learned about string children. I can't concentrate on anything else."

Pippa sighed. "Fine," she said. She picked up the old book and

147

tapped the red seal on its cover. "It's all in here," she said, brandishing the book, "if only I could understand it. So far I've got some basics: that they were first invented as training partners at one of the ancient academies; that people would create string children of their fiercest competitors, then practice against them until the real event. All fine so far, but then there's this ominous riddle about what happens when a child plays against their own double." She flipped to a page, then tilted the green book so that Legacy could read:

> *Dawn breaks, light plays;*
> *Every darkness has its day.*
> *Attack, attack!*
> *The replica's back!*
> *How can a match end between one and the same?*

Legacy furrowed her brow. What did dawn break have to do with string children? Who was supposed to attack? And how was she supposed to take anything away from a poem that ended with a question?

"Do you understand it?" Pippa said.

Legacy read it again. She tilted her head one way. She tilted it the other. Oh.

Oh.

Her mouth tasted like ash. She had hoped this would be a nice distraction from Van.

Pippa shook her head. "It sounds like a whole lot of nonsense to me," she said. "And that's not even the worst of it. Here, for instance, is some prime academic gobbledygook." She pushed the page toward Legacy:

The nature of the string child is sameness. Not exactitude, not exactly, but sameness. Especially in what is visible. {See: exteriority, that which is seen from the outside.} In all visible senses, the string child will resemble the original child. In short: a string child is a perfect replica. To all the world, the same as the original.

The ash was still in Legacy's mouth. It was hard for her to concentrate on what Pippa was saying, and not only because the syntax was contorted.

"If I understand that passage," Pippa was saying, "a child and a string child might seem to be exactly the same, but they're only the same in all *visible* senses. You look the same, you move the same, and you express the same grana. But that still leaves a lot of wiggle room. I mean, first off, you're made of flesh and blood. She's made of string. You were born. She was *made*. And I think there might be other differences also."

Pippa pointed to another passage in the green book:

An ontological study of the nature of a string child reveals the string child's lack of free will, or self-determination, e.g., the ability to choose without consulting his creator—

"Ontological?" Legacy said. She started to focus again. Maybe there was something here that would help her beat her double, help her defy that terrible poem and—

Pippa consulted the book's glossary. "Ontological: of or relating to ontology—"

Legacy rolled her eyes. "It doesn't matter. The main point is that a string child can't choose without consulting whoever it is who created him. Or her. Which, in this case, is Silla."

Pippa nodded. "So now she has to do Silla's bidding."

Anger formed into a knot in Legacy's stomach. "But how did she make this . . . string thing?!"

As soon as she said it, she recalled the string cats in Pippa's father's workshop, and she wished she'd bitten her tongue. It wasn't hard to imagine who had helped her create a string child: Pippa's father, stringer to Silla, who had woven the illegal stringbinds that nearly killed Legacy.

Legacy glanced at Pippa, hoping she hadn't heard. Pippa put her arm around Legacy's shoulder. "It's okay," she said. "My father might have made this string child, but I'm going to help you figure out how to beat her. And the answers are right here; it's just so hard to parse all the ancient language. For instance, this passage about how a string child is made: it's so snarled, I can't even bring myself to read it out loud. But the gist, it seems to me, and maybe this will help us understand her weaknesses, is that the first step in the process is to get the recipe for the real child's racket."

She looked up at Legacy. "That means yours."

Legacy nodded. "Right. Two threads of metium, six threads of cormorant feather, nine threads of owl claw, and a weft of corasite threads." Legacy would never forget her string recipe, the one that her *Book of Muse* had revealed to her. It was hers, and hers alone, and she and Pippa had found it together.

Pippa smiled. "Exactly. So, *somehow*—and we can circle back to that later—Silla must have gotten that recipe. Who knows how? It's in your *Book of Muse*, and it should only be visible to you. But regardless, she got it. And once you've got that, the next step in making a string child is weaving those particular strings into the particular shape of the real child."

Pippa looked up. "The real child," she repeated. "As in you."

Legacy nodded. "That shouldn't have been too hard. There are pictures of me everywhere."

Pippa stared down at the page in front of her. "And finally," she said, "the last step of the process, the step that brings the string child to life, is writing down what the author describes as an 'accurate—and precise—description of the original child provided by a person who loves her, see glossary for working definition of love.'"

Legacy furrowed her brow. "But what do you do with the description?"

Pippa skimmed a few more paragraphs. "It seems that you write it down on a piece of parchment, roll it up, and place it in the mouth of the string child. That brings her to life. Or at least, that's when she starts moving, and talking, and—"

"So, what this guy is saying, is that someone who loves me—and, presumably, knows me really well—described me to Silla. Truthfully and accurately. And Silla wrote that down, and that went into False Legacy's mouth?"

Pippa shrugged.

"It doesn't make sense," Legacy said.

"I know," Pippa said. "Who would have done that? And—and, anyway, how could she have gotten your string recipe?"

Legacy jumped up without saying a word and ran down the stairs to the bedroom. She got down on her knees and reached under her bed and pulled out a little wooden box. There was only one thing inside. She lifted it out and ran back to the attic, then dropped her *Book of Muse* on the dusty table.

"It's here," Legacy said. "Silla doesn't have it—and even if she did, she couldn't read it. I'm the only one who can see the writing on the pages of my book. And anyway, it's right here!" She opened the cover and began to flip through the pages, past the diagrams for proper pyrus mount, past the recipes for salves to heal grip blisters, until suddenly she stopped.

She ran her finger over the ragged edge of a torn page.

She held up the book.

Pippa gasped. "Is that—?"

There was no question. Someone had torn it out.

"Who could have done this?" Legacy cried.

Who in the world knew where it was? One of the littles? But they've been here the whole time! she thought.

"Oh—Legacy," Pippa was saying. She looked like she was on the verge of tears. "Maybe it was my father. Before we left the academy. He knew what we were up to. He must have known we'd found the recipe for your bind. He'd have known where to look. And if anyone in the republic would know how to make the pages of a *Book of Muse* visible, it would be him."

"There might be another explanation," Legacy tried.

But tears were already spilling out of Pippa's eyes. "It had to have been him. Anyone else would have taken the whole book."

Legacy gave Pippa a hug. It wasn't her fault that her father was one of Silla's stooges. "It's okay, Pippa. It doesn't matter. The bigger thing— the thing I'm more worried about—is even if they do have the recipe for my stringbind, who gave them the description? Someone who loves me. And someone who would have been willing to betray me."

"I can't imagine," Pippa said. "I can't imagine anyone—"

Then Legacy closed her eyes. There was Van again, in his scholar's robe. Standing beside False Legacy in that vision.

Legacy opened her eyes.

"Van," she breathed. "They have my recipe, and they have my best friend."

Pippa's eyes widened. "Of course!" she said. "But how could Silla have gotten him to help her create a string double of you? Why would he do that?"

Legacy shook her head. "I have no idea," she said. "But we both know that Silla is frighteningly resourceful. She must have duped him into talking about me. Telling someone everything he knows about me."

"Maybe he doesn't know that you're not False Legacy."

"Maybe he really believes that she's me."

"We should tell him," Pippa said.

"But I don't have time to get to the city before Capari," Legacy said. "And a courier's note could be intercepted—the crackles don't dare to come into the forest, but they follow all the courier routes."

"And anyway," Pippa said, "I guess the damage is done."

Legacy felt tears prick her eyes. "He can't have done it on purpose," she said, trying to persuade herself as much as anyone else. She had come to the attic for clues about False Legacy's weaknesses. Now it seemed as though she'd only revealed more of her own. Someone else had her stringbind. And her best friend had made it possible for them to use it.

"He can't have done it on purpose," Legacy whispered again. "He would never have purposefully betrayed me."

CHAPTER SIXTEEN

SILVERY STRANDS

It helped, after imagining Van helping Silla to make the string child, for Legacy to go running with Javi and Jenni. Instead of wondering whether there was any possible way that her best friend had known he was helping Silla to create a double Legacy, it helped to feel the soft forest moss underfoot. To smell the scent of cycapress. To listen for the calls of the whipwings.

To let her mind become one with her body so that her brain was full of footsteps. So that the only things that mattered were the burning in her calves and the way she pumped her arms at her sides.

They reached the court in the forest, and Legacy kept running. This was her last morning run before they left for Capari; after today, they'd start tapering her training. So with each step she took, Legacy was aware of a certain "lastness." Her last day to run in the forest. One of the last days she had to move without anyone watching.

She wanted to enjoy it. She wanted to luxuriate in the sensation.

Past the court, there were three drammus saplings that had grown up in the last months. Their yellow leaves mixed with the dark green cycapress and the pale silvery green of the cherish trees, and the early-morning sunlight filtered through them all and fell softly across Legacy's face.

The three friends moved through the meadow, spotted with pink and yellow and silver flowers. The light was still gentle, and the buzzbugs hadn't risen yet for the day. The Herman's Wingfeathers were cooing, and the blue flickerflies flitted from one fallen log to the next.

"We should stop," Javi called. "It's too close to the event for a strenuous run."

But Legacy was enjoying herself too much. She wanted to keep running.

"Just a little longer," she called. Then she lost herself again in her footsteps. This was farther than they'd ever run in this direction. Farther than she'd ever explored in the forest. So her heart started to pound in her chest when she saw the gold stand of drammus.

There must have been seven or eight of them, catching the morning light so that each tree seemed to have a gold halo. And beyond, a building—dilapidated, yes, with vines over the doors and holes in the walls and trees somehow growing out of the windows, but a building that had once been beautiful—with peaked turrets in the roof and long winding porches and windows that arched up to the eaves. And in front of the building, courts.

Legacy stopped running. Courts?

It was impossible to believe, but there they were: six or seven overgrown grass courts, with sagging nets and decomposing referee stands.

"What *is* this place?" Jenni said from behind her.

They crossed the courts and pushed their way through a rotting wood door into the building. The first room was an enormous gymnasium: everything was dusty and strewn with cobwebs, but there were the racks of medicine balls, the rows of dumbbells, the orange cones for agility drills. Legacy could smell that familiar scent of waxed cycapress wood, the same scent that had filled the gym at the academy.

"It's an academy," she said.

"What I couldn't have done with some of those dumbbells!" Javi said.

"Who built it?" Jenni said. "Why is it here? I didn't think there were any provi academies."

They moved through a room with an empty pit that seemed to have once been a whirlpool and another room with an indoor track, and finally they came to what seemed to be a locker room.

There were row upon row of lockers, but only one with a name plaque. *Petrin*, it read, the script carved into silver.

Legacy stepped forward. Her hand paused on the latch. Then she opened it.

Inside, there was a racket. It was wooden, and warped from years of moisture. And mice had nibbled holes in the strings. But when she reached behind it, there was a note:

For my wife. From her loving husband.

My father, Legacy thought. *My father wrote that note for my mother.*

"This must be the training center they started to build," Legacy said. "My father told me about it once, when I was bugging him for more stories about my mother. The court they built was just the first step. She wanted to have a whole training center for children from the

156

provinces. A place where orphaned and abandoned kids could come to learn tennis. I thought they'd only gotten as far as the court. I didn't know they'd actually built it."

Legacy closed her eyes. She remembered what her father had said on the night she'd returned from the city: *We had so much fun while we did it. We laughed together all day.*

She opened her eyes and looked around at the lockers, the dust, the cobwebs in the corners. This was the dream her mother had had. The refuge her father had wanted to build. Now, even more than those days when her mother and father had built this academy in the forest, there was a need for refuge for children from the provinces. Their parents were dying in the mines. They themselves were being lured to work in those lower levels.

Legacy looked at her friends. "This was their center. And this"— she held up the racket—"this must have been my mother's racket."

On their way out of the building, Legacy and Jenni and Javi stopped to look at the courts. One appeared to be a kind of sand court, but when Legacy stepped on it, she felt her feet sinking faster and deeper than she would have expected. Emitting a little yelp, she leaped backward. Then she tried the next court. That one was normal grass, but the net appeared to be a few feet higher than a normal net. And the dimensions of the court were a bit longer.

"What are these courts?" Jenni breathed.

"I don't know," Javi said, "but they clearly were working with some pretty innovative approaches to training."

Legacy stared at the building and the courts: the training center her parents had started but never gotten off the ground because her mother left and her father had enough on his hands keeping the orphanage open.

Jenni was nodding approvingly. "I know some kids in the mines who could use some real facilities."

Javi grinned. "And some builders who could use a little time above-ground."

"That's what my parents wanted," Legacy said. "This place was their dream. And now maybe it's mine, too."

———————

They had four days before Capari. Four days to run drills: more fore-hand drives, just like she'd done with Jenni, and backhand drives and forehand cross-courts and backhand cross-courts. And when she'd finished training with the actual ball, Javi took the ball away, and she ghosted the same drills, over and over. One, two, three: she counted her footsteps. She set her feet, she swung through the ball she could see in her mind's eye. When she'd finished cross-courts and drives, she ghosted volleys and lobs. She did them over and over again, until her mind floated away and she was no more than a body. Until she was the angle of her wrist, the grip of her hand on the racket. The placement of her feet, the depth of her lunge. She did those drills until her forearms ached as badly as they had when she was stirring the porridge. She did them with her eyes closed. She took a break to eat some of Javi's home-made energy bars. And then she got back out on court and did more drills as the sun set. She did them when starlight cast a cold pall over the court in the forest. She did them over and over again, submitting to the process. Remembering that the game was bigger than her. That all she could do was count each of her footsteps. She did them until she felt her fingers tingle and a warmth fizz at the roots of her hair, until in the darkness that had fallen over the forest, she lit her own way with the gentle glow of her grana.

Then she did them again, and when she felt her fingers tingling, she moved her racket to the other hand, blew on them, breathed the way Pippa had taught her to calm herself down, and played without grana: the way she'd have to play in Capari until she met False Legacy.

After the last day of training, carrying her mother's old racket, Legacy followed Javi and Jenni back to the orphanage. Pippa met them on the back steps. Legacy lifted her mother's racket. "Are you ready to get to work, Pip?" she said. "Because I'm going to need new strings in this racket."

First, Pippa had to mix the prosite dust into a paste, using a tiny silver mortar and pestle that she pulled out of her velvet-lined box. Once she'd done that, she rolled the paste into silvery strands, which she pulled through her perforated silver comb, turning them into strings. Jenni helped by holding the strings as they emerged out of the comb; Javi hung them like drying spaghetti over the back of one of the rickety chairs.

Then, carefully, Pippa pulled the old strings out of Legacy's Tempest. Legacy watched her anxiously.

"We'll use your regular stringbind," Pippa explained while she hung the old strands alongside the newer silvery ones. "And just add a few of these prosite strands to the weft. There aren't any dangerous side effects to adding more prosite, at least not when it's balanced. It'll reflect who you are now a little more closely. You're not the same person you were when you were at the academy. This new bind will reflect the work you've done, and the ways in which the process has changed you."

Legacy nodded. She glanced at the old racket she'd brought back from the forest. She hoped she was right to play with that one instead of the Tempest. It was a little warped and certainly contained none of the mineral technology of the Tempest. But she wanted to use a racket that was part of her, a racket that came from the same place that she came from.

While they waited for the prosite threads to dry, the four friends discussed the best way to beat False Legacy. Javi was sure it was a question of sticking with the fundamentals. Jenni thought it was a question of heart: real Legacy would want it more, and so she was sure to win. Pippa felt it had to do with mindset, and being connected to her strings, but she also felt her old book was trying to tell her something important that she hadn't quite understood yet.

"I keep going back to that rhyme," she said. "Dawn breaks, light plays, every darkness has its day—"

"Attack, attack," Legacy murmured. "I've been thinking about it, too." She fiddled with one of Pippa's little silver stringing tools. Then she changed the subject.

"But even more importantly," she said, "even if I do beat False Legacy, even if I do shine brighter than she does, are we sure that people will believe that I'm the real Legacy?"

"Of course," Javi said. "You know the saying: 'No one shines brighter than Legacy Petrin.'"

"I know," Legacy said. "But at the end of the day, it's just a saying, it's no guarantee."

Pippa sighed. "I guess that's a risk we'll have to take," she said. "If you want to get your identity back."

"And regardless of whether they know who the real Legacy is," Jenni said, in a darker tone of voice, "they'll see who the better Legacy is. And they'll prefer her. And as long as the people love you, Silla won't be able to touch you."

Pippa was nodding. "Not without risking her image on the tapestry blurring again."

"And her chances of re-election," Javi said.

Legacy nodded. "It's a good plan," she said. "Now we just have to make sure I can beat her."

Pippa tested the strings to see if they were dry, then nodded in satisfaction. She clamped Legacy's racket into place on the table.

"Okay," she said, "you know the deal. Tell me a story while I work. If I string this without your story, it'll just be strings and nothing more. I have to put you into this."

Legacy didn't know where to begin. So much had happened in the past two weeks. They'd discovered the existence of False Legacy; they'd gone to the summer carnival; they'd walked to Minori; her father had died.

Her father had died.

Legacy put her head in her hands.

A moment later, she felt Pippa's hand on her shoulder. Her friend's voice was gentle. "Any story," she said. "We gotta get going."

Uncertainly, at first, Legacy began to talk about Horzst and Illy and the purple minerals they'd grown on the ceiling of their underground house.

That made her think of the stones her father had sometimes brought back from the forest. So she told Pippa about all his collections: the forest rocks and butterfly wings, the blue wazoon feathers and pressed flowers. She told her about how her father had always loved to learn. About that boring book about pottery in Capari. About that final night: reading to her father while the life passed out of his body.

Nodding approvingly, Pippa finished the weft using the new silver strands. For the weave, she used Legacy's old strings, a blend of corasite, metium, and older prosite.

Silently Legacy watched her. Somehow, it seemed as though the life that had passed out of her father's body was passing into those strings. Now it was a racket that contained him. A racket that contained him and her mother, and wood from the forest that Legacy loved, and prosite from the mines where she'd learned to play in the darkness.

That's what she was playing for: those kids in the mines; the forest; her father. When Pippa was done, she handed Legacy her new racket. It felt light in her hands, but also heavy. Balanced. Right. A racket that had always been part of her family, but that she'd only just realized she needed.

CHAPTER SEVENTEEN

CRYSTAL AND GOLD

Jenni stayed behind to look after the orphanage. It couldn't be avoided: Hugo and Ink weren't old enough to do it on their own. And, anyway, Jenni insisted: If she went to Capari, she wasn't going as part of another player's coaching staff. She would be a competitor.

At first, Legacy refused. Jenni *was* part of her coaching staff. She had been essential to her training.

But Jenni had the last word.

"The biggest thing you can do to reward me for my help," she said, "is to win this tournament, reveal what a fraud False Legacy is, and put an end to these new mines in Minori. If I can help you do that by staying here at the orphanage, so be it."

"It's not fair," Legacy tried again. "You should—"

Jenni frowned. "No, it's not. But life's not fair. Especially when Silla has the power she does."

Legacy paused. Jenni frowned deeper. "What are you waiting for? Go play. Show your light. Let's get some change started in this country."

And so they set out: Pippa, Javi, and Legacy. Pippa had sewn a heap of Legacy's old burlap shifts into three Mino jumpsuits. They were all wearing the leather caps that Horzst and Illy had given them as going-away presents. Javi had decided he wanted his face coated in silvery dust; Pippa had chosen the rust red of metium. Legacy asked for them all, so that the apples of her cheeks and the arch of her brow shone multicolored and iridescent. They'd rubbed dust on their collarbones, on their wrist bones; they'd caked it into their nails. And finally, as a last step, Pippa had cropped Legacy's long hair.

It was strange for Legacy, looking at herself in the mirror. She didn't look like herself. She'd always had long hair. She'd never worn her burlap as a jumpsuit. She'd never been coated in shimmery dust.

But after the last two weeks, she wasn't so easy to startle. She closed her eyes. She didn't need to see herself to know who she was. She was Legacy Petrin. And she was a champion.

It was easy to find a cart that was heading for the port: anyone in the country with a little time and money to spare was heading to watch the tournament in Capari. From the open back where Legacy, Javi, and Pippa were sitting, Legacy watched the world change as they headed toward the coast: the new green trees of the regrowing forest gave way to the great black barrens from the Great Fire. That, in turn, gave way to the scrubby brown foothills of the Southern Peaks, which soared up to black spires sprinkled with snow. And finally, once the road had curved up to pass the last scrubby brown hill, there was the vast blue expanse of the sea.

The sea! She had never seen anything like it before. Neither had Javi. He kept rubbing his eyes. "Can't be real," he was muttering, under his breath.

Pippa, however, had vacationed there several times with her family, and was now pointing out features of the shore that she had learned from her father. Remembering the advantages of Pippa's other life—the luxuries she'd abandoned to follow Legacy out to the forest—always made Legacy feel a little guilty, so by the time they'd disembarked at the port and boarded a boat to the Isle of Capari, Legacy welcomed the rushing wind that came up from the sea and drowned out the sound of her friends talking.

Along with all the other excited tournament-goers, she and Pippa and Javi elbowed their way to the prow of the boat, where they stood in the spray of salt from the ocean and watched while the coast of Capari came into view.

There were the yachts of wealthy vacationers tethered in the harbor; the palm trees, waving in the blue sky; the vast white beaches; the long promenade. As the boat approached the island, Legacy glimpsed terra-cotta-tiled roofs and grand hotels with tall pink shutters, iron filigree balconies, and elaborately domed roofs. And finally, once they'd rounded a tall jag of rock, she saw the tournament grounds. A massive oval-shaped tent stood right on the beach, ringed with pennants of every color and anchored at regular points by huge flags that represented all the different provinces. There was the elegant red-and-black flag of the city, the deep green flag of the forestry province, and even the black flag embroidered with eight small circles of color that represented Minori.

Legacy, Pippa, and Javi followed the rest of the tournament-goers from the harbor into the tent, and Legacy looked around at the crowd milling between courts. There were no long swinging braids, no slick pompadours. No one was dressed like Gia anymore; no one was dressed like Villy Sal. And no one was dressed like Legacy.

The rule forbidding imitation of champions must still be well enforced, she thought. She touched her cropped hair. She hoped she was unrecognizable in her jumpsuit.

Once they'd checked in for Peg Letrin's place in the qualifying round, they headed off to find a hotel. They tried the official tournament hotel first—a grand old building on the promenade, with pink and gold domes for the roof and a black-and-white-checkerboard floor in the lobby. Nervously Legacy passed several guards in uniform. Her disguise must have worked; they let her go by without moving a muscle.

"They don't think you're you," Pippa whispered while they waited in line at the front desk, under a crystal chandelier in the shape of an octopus.

"No one thinks I'm me," Legacy whispered back.

Then she glanced around at the decor in the lobby, all crystal and gold and seashore-themed, the white sofas with seahorse jacquard, the creamy rugs threaded with gold waves, the vases in the shapes of shells. It was only when they were next in line to speak to a hotel representative that Legacy turned and saw False Legacy sitting on one of the enormous, velvet seashell-shaped chairs toward the back of the lobby.

False Legacy, and a boy who seemed to be attending her. A boy with glasses and bark-brown skin, wearing a robe and—

Van.

It was Van, sitting beside False Legacy.

He was laughing at something she'd said. His smile lit up his face. And his crooked glasses seemed to have been fixed.

Legacy stared. He thought *she* was *her*. He thought False Legacy was real. She could tell by his face: he completely believed her.

166

Legacy started toward him. He'd know. If he saw her, he'd know it was her, and—

Javi's hand was pulling her back. Pippa was hissing a warning.

"Not now," Pippa said.

"You can't afford to blow your disguise," Javi whispered.

"Not now, before the tournament's even started."

Legacy felt as though she'd swallowed a piece of prosite. Now it was stuck, cold and hard, somewhere in her chest.

Van had been her best friend. Now—from the looks of it—he was *hers*.

Standing there in the lobby, surrounded by gold and crystal, Legacy had never felt so alone. Even with Pippa and Javi beside her. She couldn't even go say hello to her friend. She couldn't even tell him her father had died.

She gave him one more glance. He looked happy. He seemed to be enjoying his time with False Legacy.

With tears blurring her vision, Legacy turned to the front desk.

"No more vacancy," the attendant was saying, looking down his nose at Legacy's burlap jumpsuit. "And if I were you, I wouldn't waste my time at any of the fine seaside hotels. It's far too late in the—"

Legacy didn't hear any more. It was all she could do to numbly follow Pippa and Javi when they headed back out to the street.

———————

The next three hotels they tried were booked. Their lobbies were crowded with people who seemed to have come from the city, wearing elaborate braids and luxurious silks. They didn't see anyone who had come from Minori or Cora or any of the other provinces.

As the friends walked farther and farther from the tournament tent, passing fish vendors and storefronts cluttered with the famous local ceramics, they began to see more and more locals, if the galoshes over their muslin trousers and vests with hundreds of tiny pockets were any sign. They also began to see more signs of disrepair. The whitewashed facades of the houses, built into the hillsides, seemed to have been damaged by wind and rain, so that they were streaked with black. The stone streets were pocked with holes. And some citizens had erected tents in little dark alleys and muddy corners.

This far from the ocean, the streets smelled like garbage and cat urine and laundry. There were tattered undershirts, muslin vests, and trousers hanging from lines threaded outside people's windows. As the three friends moved toward a somewhat grim hotel—far less glamorous than the ones they'd passed closer to the water—they heard an old woman emerging from a restaurant, yelling over her shoulder: something about city dwellers and overfishing and shortages at the market. When she saw Legacy staring, she scowled and looked suspiciously at Legacy's unfamiliar outfit. Legacy rushed into the grimy hotel, followed closely by Javi and Pippa.

The next day, from the beginning of her qualifying match, Legacy—or Peg—dominated the match. Her opponent—an academy kid, if her sleek red dress and brand-new Tempest were any indication—wasn't particularly strong. And Legacy was well prepared. In her loose burlap jumpsuit, cropped at the ankles, and her hair cropped close to her skull, Legacy moved around the court with ease. No part of her game was vulnerable: not the forehand drives she'd practiced over and over again in the forest, not the backhand cross-courts, not the volleys or the lobs. She could have played as well as she was with her eyes closed, just as she had in the forest, when she was ghosting from one corner of the court to the other.

Her main challenge was keeping her grana under wraps. She knew she couldn't let herself glow: it would have drawn too much attention to herself. But it felt so good to be out on court, to be competing again, that in the second set, despite her best efforts, her fingers started to tingle. She tried switching her racket to her other hand between points, blowing on her fingers, breathing the way Pippa had taught her to calm herself down.

But even so: she must have begun to glow slightly, because a crowd began to gather around the side court where she was playing. She could hear them whisper and murmur.

"Is that provi glowing?" she heard someone say. "Another light grana, could it possibly be?" someone chimed in. "Weak, though, of course," someone else answered. "No one shines brighter than Legacy Petrin."

Legacy glanced at Pippa and Javi up in the crowd. Pippa was shaking her head. Javi's eyes were darting around, looking to make sure—Legacy assumed—that none of Silla's officials had been around to see the faint glow.

Legacy paused and took another deep breath. She couldn't let herself glow. If she couldn't calm down, she had to throw herself off.

She thought about Van.

She thought about Van, laughing in the lobby with False Legacy.

Her fingers stopped tingling. The roots of her hair went cold.

She thought about how she had to win this tournament, if she was going to prove who she really was.

Then she felt the old weight on her shoulders. She felt herself getting pressed down. If she let her guard down, it almost seemed to her that the court was lengthening. That the net was growing.

She stopped glowing. More of her shots went long.

The match got a little closer, and by the time Legacy won it, most of the crowd had drifted off, disappointed, muttering the familiar saying: "No one shines brighter than Legacy Petrin."

CHAPTER EIGHTEEN

A FLASH IN THE PAN

That afternoon, Legacy managed two more victories without drawing too much attention to herself. Before she knew it, Pippa and Javi were ushering her toward a court at the far edge of the tournament tent for her quarterfinal match. At the same time, on court two, Sondra Domenicu was playing "Legacy Petrin."

It was that match that had drawn all the crowds. Even from her distant court, Legacy could hear people oohing and aahing, exclaiming about the light grana of Legacy Petrin. She could see Silla, sitting on a raised platform overlooking the court in her magnificent silks, flanked by two coaches from the academy: Polroy and Lucco, Pippa's father. Judging from the roaring applause, False Legacy was winning. People were stomping and calling her name. Rays of light sometimes splayed out from the court and crossed the white silk of the tent.

Given the light show that was going on there, no one cared about a match between the local star—Wick Sindril—and Peg Letrin, some unknown kid from Minori.

Before she walked on court, Pippa and Javi gave her a pep talk. "Flick Sindril's no joke," Javi said. "It'll be a challenge to beat him without using your grana."

Legacy furrowed her brow. "Flick Sindril?" She recalled the charity match in the book peddler's brochure.

Pippa also looked confused. "Isn't it Wick?"

Javi leafed through the tournament program. "Hunh," he said. "Looks like there's a Wick and a Flick Sindril. Identical twins. Both from the island. But you're playing Flick. I mean Wick. You're definitely playing Wick."

Pippa handed her a glass bottle of water. "If you beat him, you'll start attracting attention. He's a local favorite; they all expect him to win. That's fine; just make sure you stay in disguise. We can't reveal who you are until you're up against the other Legacy."

"No grana of any kind," Javi agreed.

"Just strong serves," Pippa said. "And get to the ball early."

Javi was still peering down at the program. "Looks like both Sindril twins are some of the quickest in the tournament." He started to read from the program: "Almost as though playing not one but two opponents," he said.

"Got it," Legacy said.

But Javi was still reading. "Opponents are often confused, overwhelmed, utterly devastated by the famous Sindril Twin quickness."

Legacy was beginning to feel the weight on her shoulders. "Got it!" she said, and Javi glanced up from the program.

Pippa patted her on the shoulder. "But they can't be quicker than Zaza," she said, "when she's sneaking into the pantry!"

Javi agreed. "Or than a whipwing or a buzzbug or Cora's own Legacy Petrin!"

Legacy smiled at her friends' efforts. Still, the weight on her shoulders was there. This was it. She'd have to beat Flick—or Wick; whichever it was—without any grana.

Before the match started, Legacy shook hands with Wick. He sauntered up to the net, grinning like he was sitting on some big juicy secret. Then he jogged back to the baseline, and Legacy moved to her baseline to return his serve, but stopped first to tie her shoe.

There was the sound of a bounce.

Then a call from the ref: "FIFTEEN–LOVE."

Legacy looked up from her sneaker. Her jaw dropped. Wick was plucking at his racket and getting ready to serve again.

"I'm not even ready!" Legacy shouted. The sparse crowd behind the court booed. There were a few locals sitting in clumps, drinking from flasks and cheering for their local hero. She heard cries of "Get out and play, Minori!"

So, this was how it was going to be.

She ran out to her side and returned Wick's second serve with ease. He didn't have much power, but he was just as quick as she was, and the second point of the match turned into a rally that felt almost endless.

She was already breathing heavily by the time that she was able to pin him to his backhand corner, then drop a shot just over the net for a winner.

"FIFTEEN ALL!" came the shout from the ref.

Still keeping herself from glowing too much, Legacy managed to eke out a win in the first game. But she was exhausted. The points were going on forever. This was going to be a very long match.

Switching sides between games, Legacy grabbed a towel from Pippa and wiped the sweat from her forehead. "Well, at least he doesn't seem to have any grana," Javi whispered from his spot behind her bench.

Legacy jogged back to the baseline and waited for the serve. Javi was right. It didn't seem like Wick had any grana, as far as she could tell. But then again, neither did she. Theirs was going to be a totally regular tennis match. It was almost a relief, except she didn't know how Wick had so much endurance.

She looked over to his side of the court, where he was still on the bench. Flick was there, too, re-taping his brother's racket. They really did look identical, and they were wearing the exact same white shorts and pale purple shirt.

Then Wick grabbed the racket from Flick and walked back to his spot.

At least, she *assumed* it was Wick.

The next game went even longer than the first. They rallied back and forth so long that the crowds in the stands got quiet and fidgety. They could hear the other sections—people were still stomping and calling Legacy's name—but in the distant quarter of the main tent where Peg Letrin and Wick Sindril were playing, it was practically silent, save for the thwacks and thuds of the ball and their rackets.

At one point, as she scrambled backward to get to a shot Flick had tried to lob over her head, Legacy could even hear some muttering from the sparse locals who were watching the match.

"Is this really all she has?" she heard someone say.

"Does she even have any grana? She looks tired," someone responded.

"Flash in the pan," another agreed.

Legacy winced. She hadn't even flashed yet. But they were right: she *was* tired. This match had hardly started, and it already felt like she'd been playing for an eternity. Her right calf was threatening to cramp up, and as she bent down to stretch it out for a split second, she heard a *whoosh* followed by "GAME: WICK SINDRIL." She whipped her head up in astonishment. How had he gotten to that return so quickly? Wick was smiling and bouncing on his heels. He wasn't even sweating.

Between games, Flick came out and re-gripped Wick's racket. Once again, they huddled for a moment, and then Wick retreated to the stands, and Flick trotted on court and got ready to serve.

Wick, that is, Legacy corrected herself.

Or: wait a minute.

Just as he was lifting the ball to toss it in the air, Legacy called out, "Hey, Wick!"

Both brothers turned toward her and responded, in unison, "What?"

Then the one on the court angrily turned to the one on the sideline and shushed him.

They were swapping in for each other!

She'd been playing them both. Legacy glanced up at the referee in his stand. He had to have noticed. They were barely disguising it. She had worked so hard to get here, and she had made promises: to her friend Jenni Bruno, not to mention the littles. And now she wasn't even going to get a chance to play False Legacy and reveal Silla's manipulations to the people of Nova, because these two jokers were cheating.

It wasn't fair. Why was everyone here, everyone in the whole country, so determined to put her back in her place?

Legacy's fingertips starting fizzing. The roots of her hair were hot. And then—before she could do anything about it, light was shooting out from her body.

Wick's and Flick's faces fell. They finally stopped grinning. Legacy twirled her new wooden racket in her left hand. When she next served, a ray of light shot up toward the clouds that had drifted over the Isle of Capari.

The small crowd let out a roar. Finally, a show.

"Light grana!" she heard someone shout.

Groaning, Legacy switched her racket to her other hand. She blew on her fingers. This wasn't the plan. She was meant to stay in disguise and not reveal her grana until she was playing False Legacy.

She looked down at her arm, sheathed in the burlap of her jump-suit. She ran her fingers through her newly cropped hair. She'd have to hope that her costume was enough to prevent anyone thinking that she was Legacy Petrin.

Or—worse—an illegal imitation of Legacy Petrin.

———

By the end of the match, the two brothers weren't even bothering to hide their cheating. They ran across the court and even started to both play at the same time, but it was too late. They were both winded, and neither could consistently get to Legacy's blistering returns. Her light had reared up around her in an enormous, glowing halo, and the twins kept losing sight of the ball. It didn't help that there were two of them, if neither one of them could return the shots she was hitting.

Though they'd been against her at first, by the final points of the match, the crowd had turned. They were roaring for her, roaring for Peg Letrin, this new girl from Minori whose grana—she heard a few times—was "almost as strong as Legacy Petrin's."

After she'd won, she met Pippa and Javi back in the hotel room. Javi gave her an energy bar. Pippa rubbed her aching shoulders.

"Well," Javi said, "you didn't listen to our advice about not sum-moning grana."

"You'll have to be more careful," Pippa said, "tomorrow, when you play Gia."

"Gia?" Legacy murmured.

Pippa nodded. "She won her match, too. That's who you'll play in the semifinals."

Legacy closed her eyes. For a moment, she was back in the finals of the nationals. Gia's darkness had whirled up and surrounded the court, leaking over the sidelines like ink spewed by an octopus. It had permeated the stadium where they were playing; bats had flown out of the ramparts. It had felt as though the darkness would sweep through her, carry her off in its current. It had felt as though she'd lose herself. Only by summoning grana had she been able to push back against all that darkness. But this time she couldn't do that. She'd simply have to stand firm and allow Gia's darkness to swallow her.

She opened her eyes. Pippa smiled. "As long as you know who you are," she said, "you won't get lost in Gia's darkness."

"And as long as you stick to the process," Javi said. "Remember how hard you've worked for this. Your body knows what it needs to do. You've put in the sweat. You've done the reps."

"Sweat and reps," Legacy said in her best imitation of Javi, and even Javi had to laugh before jumping into a lecture about all the reasons to keep her grana a secret: to keep herself in disguise, to avoid recognition, to prevent Silla from having any reason to arrest her as an impersonator.

Legacy nodded as Javi ticked off the reasons. She knew he was right. She knew Pippa was right as well. But that didn't keep the fear from gnawing at the edges of her mind. It didn't keep the knot from forming in her stomach.

CHAPTER NINETEEN

SHE KNOWS

There were no spidery lines on the ceiling of her room in the hotel, like back in her room at the orphanage. So, instead, Legacy imagined they were there.

She imagined, too, that her father was in the next room, softly snoring and waiting—as he'd taken to doing in the last months—for the breakfast rush to recede so that he could sneak into the kitchen and eat his porridge in peace.

She imagined Gus was outside, standing alert and pawing the garden grass, waiting for the littles to get up so he could start playing with them.

Then she imagined all of that going away.

Some of it already had.

She imagined darkness spreading from Silla's palace, and from the metium-encrusted depths of Minori. She closed her eyes and imagined that darkness covering up the forest, the orphanage, Gus . . .

And then she got up, made her bed, dressed in her burlap jumpsuit, rubbed some shimmery dust on her face, and re-gripped her wooden racket with a roll of shiver bark.

She was ready to play her semifinal match against Gia.

As she emerged from the locker room and onto the playing floor, the clamor was overwhelming. She could make out shapes of struggling bodies and clashing groups in the stands. People were shouting, and from all directions came the competing chants. Some for Gia. Some for Silla herself. Some for Legacy Petrin. None for Peg Letrin.

"Focus on the process," Javi whispered.

"Listen to your body," Pippa whispered.

Then Legacy was alone. She counted her steps to the court. She felt her grip on her racket. She imagined herself ghosting, back in the forest, while twilight fell and the Herman's Wingfeathers began to sing their evening songs.

But the calm didn't last long.

"TO ALL ASSEMBLED," the pre-match announcer blared through a loudspeaker larger than his body. Then something about the semi-finals, and Minori, and introducing Peg Letrin.

Some scattered shouts of support came trickling down from the high seats.

The announcer gestured at her. Legacy took her place at her bench. Then the lights went out.

Legacy thought she'd fainted at first. She blinked and saw a single bright light off in the distance, wavering slightly. A white circle of light, in which a few dark shapes appeared to be approaching the floor.

"PLEASE STAND FOR THE ARRIVAL OF THE HIGH CONSUL."

The little illuminated group reached the floor, and gradually, one by one, stadium lights were switched on from high up in the dark reaches of the tent. The court and its surroundings were bathed in harsh white light, the kind that somehow still made things seem half-lit and sharper than normal.

There was Silla—as beautiful and frightening as Legacy remembered her. She was draped in her signature, rust-red silks, her tawny skin radiant, gold beads in her braids. When she sat, she waved her elegant wave, and the gold rings on her fingers glinted. Beside her, False Legacy, wearing her signature burlap shift, her hair unbraided and curly. And to her other side, Van.

Legacy stared. Yes, that was him. Her Van. Van from the orphanage. Standing beside Silla.

Why would Silla bring False Legacy? Why would she bring Van? Was it to show that she had friends from the provinces? Was it to get under Legacy's skin?

Legacy touched her cropped hair. But she wasn't Legacy. She was Peg Letrin, from Minori.

The realization made her feel a little dizzy.

False Legacy looked more like her than she did.

Silla nodded to the crowd, waved in each direction, and then stepped aside to reveal her most favored player, and Legacy's semifinal opponent.

Gia trotted out. The crowd roared. Gia waved and smiled. She looked confident, loose, her blond braid swinging. For all she knew, she was playing an unseeded, unknown, Peg Letrin from the provinces.

Legacy took her place on the baseline. A few people from the crowd started jeering. Legacy understood. As far as they all knew, she was some upstart from Minori, wearing a burlap jumpsuit and preparing to face the best player not named Legacy Petrin that anyone in the country could remember. What they wanted was a show—colored lights; shapes in the snow; a truly haunted darkness—and they didn't believe she could give them that.

Legacy bent her knees. She swayed in place, waiting for Gia's serve. No one in the stands, she realized, thought she could win. For the first time in weeks, that weight of expectation didn't press on her shoulders.

Gia's first serve was hit hard—and straight down the middle. Legacy barely had to move to return, and she didn't put her full strength into it. It might be useful, she thought, to let Gia persist in underestimating her for a while.

At thirty–love, the crowd began to get restless. She heard someone shout, "Where's your pickax, provi?" Then she heard another person scream, "Go back to the mines!" Legacy's shoulders were so light she almost felt as if she were growing. As if the court were shortening. As if the net were shrinking.

Not "as if"—they *were*. Legacy was playing on a steadily contracting court. Maybe this was a new part of Gia's grana?

Gia served again, and Legacy set her feet and swung, trying to be careful not to overhit for the new size of the court, aware that her shot might fly long until—it hit the net.

So did her next shot, and the next. She lost that game, and the next one as well, her serves barely tipping over the net, if they made it at all.

What was happening?

Wildly she glanced at Javi and Pippa. They seemed dismayed. Where had her power gone? It was as if it had been sapped from her body.

Javi was making some sort of weird ecstatic motion, moving his arms in a circle. Legacy lost the next point. She looked back at Javi. He was still circling his arms—some sort of new fist pump? An extremely awkward way of miming a boxing match?

No. Legacy started to smile.

He was stirring the porridge.

He was reminding her to get back to the process.

Before Gia's next serve, Legacy closed her eyes. *Listen to your body*, she reminded herself. Just: *listen*.

With her eyes closed, she could hear Gia bounce the ball before she served. She could hear Gia toss the ball up. She could hear it strike her strings. Two side steps, a lunge. The right tilt of her wrist.

Then Legacy swung. There was the *ping* of the shot on her strings. Then there was a murmur of surprise in the crowd. It had been a good shot. They hadn't believed she could do that.

Legacy played the next two points with her eyes closed. She won them both. By the end of the second, she was getting into such a familiar routine that she started to feel the tips of her fingers tingling. The roots of her hair were warm.

Her eyes flew open. She glanced at Pippa and Javi. Both of them were gesturing wildly. The crowd had started to cheer.

Peg Letrin from Minori was glowing.

Across the net, Gia was seething, and muttering curses to herself.

The announcer picked up his loudspeaker and shouted over the ref. "POINT: PEG LETRIN!"

Legacy couldn't help smiling. She tried to find Silla's face on the sideline, but as she turned, she was suddenly pushed to her knees from behind by a cold wind. She gasped for breath. The light funneled out of the tent. Then the crowd blinked out of existence. She was alone on a court immersed in total darkness.

She scrambled to her feet—then kicked around in circles, trying to find her racket. She heard a ball sail past her.

"POINT: GIA!"

Legacy tripped over her racket. She picked it up. She scrambled to the baseline to return the next serve, but she was off-balance. The darkness seemed to be darker than it was when she closed her eyes. She didn't have control over this. She couldn't open her eyes to end the darkness.

Gia's next serve whizzed past her as well. Then it was game point, and Legacy barely managed to return the serve, to regain the T, only to hear an overhead slam whistle by her left ear, as close as one of Gus's body shots.

She'd lost the game.

Shakily, feeling her way through the darkness, Legacy switched sides.

"Stir your porridge!" Legacy heard Javi from the sideline.

"I can't," she hissed. "It's so dark I can't even—"

"*Stir* your *porridge!*" Javi shouted again.

Legacy swallowed her nervous response.

She was panicked. But that was fine, she said to herself. That was something that happened. And what do you do? You keep stirring.

She made her way to the other side of the court. She adjusted her strings.

"She can't stand up to a real player's grana," someone said in the stands.

"Go back to Minori!" someone else shouted.

Legacy ground her teeth. All those days of training, freeing herself from high expectations: what a waste! Nobody here thought she could beat Gia. Nobody here thought she had any grana. Because she was from Minori. Because she hadn't trained in the city. Because she hadn't had all the opportunities that someone from the city—

Legacy felt herself getting angry. Her throat was tightening. Once again, her fingers were starting to tingle.

It was only faint: just light enough to see her hand bouncing the ball, the ball rising up in the air, and her wooden racket rising to meet it.

It landed on Gia's side—and came immediately back. It wasn't alone. Flying alongside it in the darkness were ribbons of cloud. One had Van's face. Beside him was False Legacy. Smiling, grinning, keeping her calm. Telling Legacy she was a flash in the pan.

It was just the same, but this time Legacy was prepared. She'd seen this before.

She'd seen those images in the mines. She'd seen them in her nightmares.

Legacy swung. The ball pinged off her strings, a blistering cross-court that didn't come back.

Legacy smiled. So this was what Javi meant when he talked about reps.

Nothing was new. Everything was familiar.

And she was prepared for this.

She was in control of this darkness.

With her eyes closed, she felt the fuzz of the ball in her hand. She counted the fractions of a second after she tossed it up. Then she bent her knees. She arched her back. Her racket flew up over the ball she'd tossed into the darkness.

Even with her eyes closed, she could hear that the ball had hit the center of the strings. She could feel the rightness in every bone of her body.

Same with her next shot, and the next, and the next after that. No matter whether her eyes were opened or closed. No matter whether Gia hit to her forehand or backhand, no matter whether Legacy was moving up to volley or running back for a lob: she had the feel of it in her body. She'd hit these shots over and over again in her mind. She didn't have to think; her muscles were already moving in the right direction.

This was the game she knew. She'd learned it doing drills in the forest.

Once she'd won that point, she won the game, and the next game after that. Her grana was strong, illuminating Gia's darkness, but more than that, her rhythm was right. She moved side to side with the grace she'd practiced under the drammus trees in the forest, chasing down a ball she'd only imagined.

She sprinted forward as though the clay courts of Capari were moss under her feet. When her strings made contact with the ball, they sang like the whipwings flying through the cherish trees.

Gia was panting in exhaustion, and Legacy could see Silla's face beyond her: curiously cool, one eyebrow arched. *She knows who I am*, Legacy thought, and for a moment the realization knocked the wind out of her chest. But then she found Pippa and Javi—they were grinning and jumping around—and finally she heard the announcer shouting through his loudspeaker.

"—CONCLUDES THE MATCH. VICTORY PEGACY LETRIN. TOMORROW WE SHALL SEE THE FINAL BETWEEN PEG LETRIN OF MINORI AND OUR OWN LEGACY PETRIN—"

CHAPTER TWENTY

EVERY DARKNESS
HAS ITS DAY

That night, Pippa convinced them to not return to the hotel deep in Capari. Legacy was exhausted and ready to collapse into bed, but Pippa made the good point that Peg Letrin was now at the center of the universe. She had, no doubt, attracted Silla's attention, and who knew what Silla would get up to.

"She knows," Legacy said. "This disguise isn't fooling her."

Javi looked at her. "What makes you say that?"

"I saw her face. I could just tell. Certainly she knows now, and maybe she knew all along. Why else would she have brought Van to the match?"

"Yes, but then why would she have allowed you to get so far without trying to stop you? Arrest you, or send one of her agents—"

"Who knows?" Legacy said. The words of that strange little poem were murmuring in her ears. *Dawn breaks, light plays, every darkness has its day . . .*

"Regardless," Pippa was saying, "we'll have to be careful. We know what Silla's capable of. She has agents everywhere, and she can make something look like an accident—"

In the end, they decided that instead of heading back to the hotel, they'd sneak into the locker room and wait for the crowds to clear out of the tent. When the janitors came through, they all hid in separate lockers and waited for the lights to go off. For a moment, when the darkness swept through the locker room, Legacy's heart lurched: this, again. Would she survive it? The eerie words of that poem echoed in her head: *Attack, attack, the replica's back.* A shadow crossed Legacy's mind.

But it was only a few seconds until the shapes of the towels and the showerheads and the lockers made themselves known. She'd found her way through an extraordinary darkness. This normal darkness was nothing.

When it was safe for them to emerge from their lockers, they gathered as many clean towels as they could find and put together a nest. Legacy lay down and fell asleep almost immediately as Pippa and Javi traded off keeping watch at the door and guarding her racket.

When Legacy woke, she looked at the clock on the locker-room wall. Two hours until her match against False Legacy. Javi distributed three of his homemade energy bars. Legacy yawned and stretched while Pippa—who was unusually silent—shook out the burlap shift she'd brought from the orphanage. Legacy dressed in her familiar outfit, wiped the last vestiges of mineral dust off her face and her arms, and finally picked up her wooden racket.

Her hair was still cropped short, but there she was. It was unmistakable. She wasn't Peg Letrin anymore. Now she was Legacy Petrin.

"This is it," Javi said in an exuberant voice. "We're going to show everyone who the real Legacy is. We're going to show everyone that you don't have to train at the academy to be a champion. We're going to introduce them to Javi and Pippa's Way: Reps and Sweat and Meditation. Listening to Your Body. Right, Pip?"

Pippa was biting her lip, staring at Legacy in the mirror. "I just wish we knew what that rhyme meant," she said. "You know: *Dawn breaks, light plays*?"

Legacy sighed. She'd been trying to banish those words from her head since she first saw the poem. Now maybe it was time to confront them.

She took a piece of parchment and a nubbin of charcoal out of Pippa's stringing kit. She tried to use her gentlest voice.

"Write it out, Pip," she said. "The way it's written in the book."

Pippa looked at her, confused, then took the nubbin and wrote. She held the parchment up.

DAWN BREAKS, LIGHT PLAYS;
EVERY DARKNESS HAS ITS DAY.
ATTACK, ATTACK!
THE REPLICA'S BACK!
HOW CAN A MATCH END BETWEEN ONE AND THE SAME?

"Do you see anything?" Legacy said.

Pippa furrowed her brow, then shook her head.

"Look at the first letters of each line," Legacy said. "What do they spell?"

Javi had come over to join them. He was looking over Legacy's shoulder. His face was still exuberant, until, suddenly, it wasn't.

"Death," he murmured.

Pippa grew pale. "Death for whom?"

Javi got that stubborn, angry expression on his face. "That can't be right," he said. "Why would we listen to some stupid old book—"

Tears were spilling out of Pippa's eyes. "Some stupid old book that's been right about everything else involved with string children!" she said. "Some stupid old book that's all we have—"

Legacy nodded. "It all fits, Javi," she said. "In the old book they talked about how the technology was used for players to practice against replicas of their opponents. But it was considered far too dangerous for a player to try to compete against a replica of herself. I don't know how it works—what happens, who dies, or how—but to me it makes sense: there can't be two of us. One of us has to prove that she's real."

Javi was silent for a while. His voice was grave when he spoke next. "So this was Silla's plan," Javi said. "This was her plan, all along."

"You can't do it, Leg," Pippa said. "It's far too dangerous—"

But Legacy cut her off. "You know what's too dangerous?" she said. "Silla's new initiatives in the mines. The new initiatives she's sure to bring to the forest. I won't let Hugo and Ink grow up in a world where Silla's word goes unchallenged. And I don't want to live in the shadow of a false version of me."

Pippa nodded. Then she squeezed Legacy's hand, and Javi turned away so quickly Legacy wondered whether he was hiding the fact that he'd started to cry.

Legacy gave herself one more look in the mirror. Even with her cropped hair, she looked like herself. She *was* herself. She wasn't going to lose to a fake Legacy Petrin.

Still, however, on her way out of the locker room, she paused for a moment. "You guys will keep the orphanage going, right? If . . . if I lose? You'll look after the littles? And make sure Gus gets his feed? And—"

She trailed off. She felt Pippa's and Javi's arms around her. Then, finally, she freed herself. It was time to go play Legacy Petrin.

CHAPTER TWENTY-ONE

LEGACY VS. LEGACY

Out on the floor, the clamor was back. It was even noisier than yesterday. And, once again, Silla's guards were rushing around, barking commands, trying to keep order.

Legacy had draped a towel over her head and moved through the crowd with her face down, hoping no one would recognize her. The tent was packed: city dwellers in their luxurious silks, but also locals from Capari wearing their galoshes and their caps with earflaps. And people had come from other parts of the country, too: suddenly, for the first time, Legacy saw families in the burlap shifts worn in Cora, and families with the coiled braids worn in the agricultural province. Perhaps, Legacy thought, it was too expensive for them to stay in Capari overnight, so they'd just come for the finals. Or maybe they'd heard that a girl from the provinces had beaten Gia again. Maybe, Legacy realized, they were here to support her.

The thought made her feel less afraid when she saw Silla—regal in her rust-red silks; elegant and murderous—glide into her box. There were other important-looking people moving into other boxes. Legacy recognized them but couldn't place them, until suddenly she remembered: the tapestry.

Those were the other figures on the tapestry. Senators, representing other provinces beyond the city. There was the senator from Capari, a short man with blue-black skin wearing a pair of sea-blue-dyed muslin trousers and a sea-blue-dyed cap. And there was the senator from Minori, a tall woman with freckled brown skin who kept her hair cropped short and wore an elegantly styled jumpsuit.

All at once, a huge mob of identically uniformed workers emerged and flooded the arena floor. They rolled up all the nets, broke apart all the referee chairs, and swept away all the detritus left by the spectators on the sidelines. It was almost as though someone had decided that match couldn't go on.

As though Silla had given up on her plan, and everyone would simply go home.

Suddenly, however, a huge metallic clatter echoed throughout the tent, and then a squeaking and squealing started to emanate from high above. Legacy looked up and, squinting against the bright klieg lights hanging from the ribs of the tent, watched as a huge slab of rectangular wood started to descend from four thick chains hooked to its four corners.

It was a tennis court—in the sky.

For a moment, the commotion in the crowd died of its own accord, the spectators held in silent rapture while the court lowered from above. Finally, when the chains stopped moving and the vast wooden slab settled into place, swinging only slightly from side to side, the whole tent erupted into whoops of excitement and applause.

Then the lights went out in the tent. The crowd disappeared. The only illuminated space was the court, made bright by a single patch of sunlight that came in through a hole in the tent. The crowd hushed, then erupted into even louder applause.

Silla knew how to serve spectacle to her subjects, that was for sure.

A rope ladder dropped from the court. She and False Legacy would be expected to climb it.

This was it, Legacy thought. This was her chance. Legacy moved toward the ladder, then felt someone shoulder past her.

There she was: False Legacy. Just a couple feet in front of Legacy.

Close enough to embrace. Close enough to clobber with her racket. She hadn't prepared for this moment.

This close, Legacy could see how similar they really were. False Legacy had the same brown skin, the same loose hair she once had, the same burlap shift she once wore, the same strong shoulders. But there were differences, too: the shift, up close, appeared to be carefully tailored, with complicated stitches at the seams. Her brown eyes were strangely glassy. And her hair only seemed loose: as False Legacy passed, it didn't move with her.

"I know what you are," Legacy whispered. "I know you aren't real. Not really."

False Legacy turned and smiled. "Oh, but I'm real!" she said. "You're the impostor!" Then she started climbing the ladder.

The crowd roared as False Legacy finished her climb and moved onto the court. She stood, waved, smiled at the crowd, and their applause surged as if in an enormous wave.

"Ladies and gentlemen," Paula Verini called into the loudspeaker. "Here we have Legacy Petrin of Cora, our national champion, beloved of the whole country!"

Below the illuminated court, Legacy swallowed. Then she followed her double. She climbed the rope ladder, and when she pulled herself up onto the court, the noise in the tent went suddenly silent.

Legacy stood. She brushed off her burlap shift. She stared into the black void that was the crowd, showing herself to them: the real Legacy Petrin.

She was greeted with silence. And darkness.

She glanced up at the announcers.

"Ladies and gentlemen," Paula said, "it appears . . ."

Then she trailed off. Angelo stepped in. "Peg Letrin appears to be dressed as Legacy Petrin—"

"We seem to have a case of illegal impersonation," Paula said. Then she glanced over at Silla's box.

Silla stood. Once again, the crowd cheered. But then: Legacy could also hear a few boos emerge from the darkness. They grew, louder and louder: almost as loud as the cheers. Legacy smiled to herself. They had come to support her. Their support would make it harder for Silla to arrest her.

Now Silla took up a loudspeaker of her own. "It appears that—in contradiction of our national law prohibiting the impersonation of our champions—'Peg Letrin' from the provinces is impersonating Legacy Petrin. Arrest her immediately for—"

She was cut off by the crowd's response. There were cheers, yes. But then also boos and shouts of protest rained down onto the court. It was audacious, but the darkness in the tent must have given the assembled spectators some confidence.

Silla's gaze—fixed on Legacy—didn't waver. And then she started to smile.

She was expecting this, Legacy realized. She'd planned on it. She wanted the match to continue. Once again, the words of that poem echoed in Legacy's ears: what happens when a match ends between one and the same.

"Ah," Silla was saying, "it appears that the people want to see the match!"

Cheers rose in the tent. False Legacy was waving and smiling to the crowd.

"I am here to serve the people!" Silla said. "Let them compete, if that's what the people wish." The crowd roared. Silla smiled. "It appears that the identity of the true Legacy Petrin is in some question. This, of course, is precisely why we issued the decree against impersonation of our champions: to avoid this kind of confusion. But someone chose to disregard that decree, and so here we are. Very well, then. You came for an exciting match. My champion won't disappoint. Everyone knows that the true Legacy Petrin—my own Legacy Petrin—has inimitably powerful light grana. What is the saying? 'No one shines brighter than Legacy Petrin'? Let's see, then, shall we? Who is the true Legacy, and who is the impostor? Let the brightest player win."

And with that, Silla sat, and the crowd roared its approval.

Legacy swallowed, brushed off her shift once again, then headed to her bench and pulled out her wooden racket. From the court, she couldn't see anyone in the crowd. She could see only the announcers, on their illuminated stand, and Silla's illuminated box.

There, beside her, were Lucco and Polroy. A few other city dwellers in elaborate silks. And one boy in a scholar's robe.

Legacy felt tears prick her eyes.

Van. Their eyes met. His brow was furrowed, behind his new glasses. His head shook side to side, almost imperceptibly. He seemed ready to say her name . . . until suddenly Silla leaned over and whispered something into his ear.

Legacy blinked back her tears.

She couldn't afford to be emotional. Not now. Not with what was riding on this. Now was the time for her to return to her process.

Legacy stood and walked out to her side of the court. She bent her knees. She swayed, waiting for False Legacy's serve.

So this is it, Legacy thought. *Legacy versus Legacy.*

When False Legacy served, her technique was beautiful. She waited, strength coiled in her body, until the ball reached its highest peak. Then she unfurled her arm, swinging over the ball with such power and grace that Legacy marveled: *Perfect form*, she thought. *More perfect than my own. Just as her shift is like mine but more elegant.*

She felt a flash of white heat before her eyes automatically shut. She fell to the ground and heard the tennis ball whoosh overhead and careen off her side of the court and into the darkness beyond.

"Point, Legacy Petrin!" Angelo cried.

"Our Legacy," Paula clarified, gesturing toward False Legacy. "As opposed to this new Legacy."

False Legacy's grana—which spread from her in a halo as soon as she struck the ball—was so bright it was blinding.

Her next serve had the same effect. It made it seem as though Legacy's side of the court was cloaked in darkness.

"It seems clear," Paula was saying, "that our Legacy has a stronger light grana than the new Legacy!"

The crowd, invisible below her, was roaring, sound moving across them in waves that Legacy couldn't distinguish. Were they roaring for her? Or for the other Legacy?

The white light that had blazed out of False Legacy's body had begun to dissipate. Legacy got to her feet. Aiming to the other service box, her counterpart was, as always, smiling. Flutters and fragments of her light grana floated around her body and blinked out of existence.

It was no use. False Legacy had everything she had but more. She was the ultimate version of . . . her. False Legacy would win this match, and when she won, well: Legacy had always known what that rhyme meant.

Walking to the other side of the baseline, her vision blurred. Another serve, another ace. Her string child won the first game.

Legacy wiped her face, headed to her bench near Silla's box, and suddenly was staring into Van's eyes. He was flush. He'd been cheering. He looked nothing like himself, and yet he also looked exactly the same: the same boy with the crooked glasses and the limp who had followed her around the orphanage. And he didn't recognize her.

Legacy stood, and on her side of the court False Legacy stood as well, and it was then that Legacy heard a commotion in the crowd. Someone was climbing the rope ladder, and then someone was running toward False Legacy, shouting something about how *she* was impersonating Legacy.

The spectator had begun pushing False Legacy, who was taken by surprise, and before Legacy knew what she was doing, she'd run over to that side of the court and pulled him off False Legacy. Then Silla's guards arrived and were hauling the spectator away, and for a moment Legacy felt sorry for him: he was dressed in burlap and clearly agitated, and she'd helped to hand him over to the authorities.

But False Legacy—false as she was—had looked so surprised, so frightened, even, by the attack that Legacy felt sorry for her. She'd wanted to help her.

Now Silla was calling for order, and Paula and Angelo were

announcing the change of sides, and as Legacy glanced back one last time at Van, she saw something change in his face.

It was doubt. He'd seen something he knew. Someone he knew.

Legacy felt a weight lift off her shoulders.

Van was looking at her. He *knew* her.

Standing on the baseline, she ran her fingers over the strings of her old, battered wooden racket: minerals from Minori. She placed her right hand on the handle: shiver bark wood from the forest. Her hands—those long fingers—she'd inherited from her father. This was her mother's racket. She knew who she was as well.

She closed her eyes and remembered the feeling of jogging through the forest with Javi. The colors of the trees returning. The forest reviving, even in the wake of her father's death. Then she reached into her pocket and touched the fragment of cherish wood. You choose goodness, her father had said. She heard his voice. And she felt herself rising taller in the darkness.

It was up to her to prove to the people of this country that she was the real Legacy. That she didn't support Silla's initiatives. That there were better ways of leading this country.

It would be up to her to build the academy her parents had started. She'd do it. She knew she could do it.

She threw the ball in the air, and as it rose, she was back in the darkness of the mines, playing against Jenni. She closed her eyes. She breathed in. She returned to her body. And when the ball reached its apogee, she swung her racket down hard. It flew past False Legacy's backhand.

When her string child recovered herself, she was no longer smiling.

Legacy won the second game. Between games, False Legacy took thirsty gulps from her bottle of water. She didn't look quite so put together anymore. One sleeve of her shift had frayed. And a few strands of her hair were out of place.

Legacy won the third and the fourth as well. She was in total control. False Legacy's face was still composed, but her hair was a mess, and some of the threads at the hem of her shift had worked themselves loose, making her look bedraggled.

Legacy noticed that, then reminded herself to keep focused. *Stir the porridge*, she said to herself. It was as easy as breathing, as practiced as walking.

When False Legacy pounded the ball to Legacy's backhand, Legacy's limbs followed the patterns of ghosting before she'd had time to think. She knew each angle of the court. No shot was farther away than the imaginary shots she'd retrieved in the forest.

When False Legacy lobbed over Legacy's head, Legacy's limbs could recall overheads she'd slammed with her eyes closed. She'd seen this lob in her mind's eye. She'd crushed her return.

She saw False Legacy's drop shots before they'd even been hit. She knew when False Legacy was planning to move to net because, well: she was also Legacy.

Legacy was playing as well as she ever had. She was stirring the cauldron. She was ghosting with Javi in the forest. She was playing with her eyes closed in the mines.

Meanwhile, her perfect string child was . . . malfunctioning.

There was no other way to put it. By the time Legacy had won the first set, Legacy wondered if there was something wrong with False Legacy. At first Legacy thought that maybe her dress was unraveling: a long brown thread trailed behind her while she switched sides between games.

Then Legacy realized: *she* was unraveling.

With every game she lost, False Legacy was unraveling further. Now her shoulders had started to droop, and her facial features had become strange. She started limping as though one of her hips had come out of joint.

"It's— Could it be?" Angelo said in amazement.

Paula looked fearful. She kept glancing at Silla. Legacy refused to follow her glance. She needed to stay focused.

"It seems that our Legacy—or Old Legacy, or perhaps we should say Legacy of the City—it seems that she has begun to come apart," Angelo said. In his excitement, he pulled his old flask out of his pocket. "This is unheard of, something I've never seen! Of course we have heard stories, banned stories, stories of Ancient Stringing Craft. String doubles, and what might happen when a string child played her double—"

He went on, but Legacy wasn't listening.

The crowd was roaring, but Legacy wasn't listening.

She was stirring the cauldron. She was ghosting, only this time it was against a real opponent. She was counting her footsteps; she was feeling each roll from heel to toe; she was transferring her weight; she was flicking her forearm. She was listening to her body.

"It's that kind of consistency," Angelo said, "that makes you think maybe she's the true Legacy."

Her body was responding. And not only by moving with more ease and swinging through with more strength: now the roots of her hair tingled, and her fingers were warm, and light—a gentle light, but a strong light—was radiating out of her body.

"And that kind of grana," Paula said.

The crowd hushed. Aiming to the other service box, Legacy saw her light rolling yellow across the white silk tent, as though the sun were shining and stretching its rays across the olive groves: she had become as bright as the sun.

The glare from her grana seemed to have blinded False Legacy, because she missed one serve, then the next. Now False Legacy's grana seemed to be escaping from her seams. She was leaking bright light: from her jawbone, from her shoulder blades, from both of her ears. Now, finally, in the last game of the match, her unspooling had begun to happen more and more rapidly.

Legacy was finding it easier and easier to score points. She took the last point with a simple drop shot, and when she moved to return it, False Legacy collapsed in a pool of multicolored threads.

The crowd erupted.

And it was only then that Legacy—the only Legacy—looked around and realized what had just happened.

"The one and only Legacy Petrin!" Angelo shouted from the stand.

"She's won again," Paula said. She seemed to have forgotten her fear of Silla. "This truly is our champion!"

Legacy heard the screech of enormous hinges, the clinking of chains, and—with a great series of lurches—she felt the court lowering into the crowd. Now people were swarming the court: reporters, officials, guards, fans. Someone she didn't know touched Legacy's hand. Someone else clawed at the hem of her shift. Pippa was standing in front of Legacy, trying to fend off reporters who got too close. It was Javi who grabbed the loudspeaker from Paula and thrust it in Legacy's face.

Legacy held on to its handle. Her throat was dry. She didn't know what to say.

Still, however, she lifted the loudspeaker to her lips.

"Whatever . . . whatever I may have said in the past," she started, then licked her lips. At the front of the crowd, she saw a little girl, wearing burlap and clutching a miniature stuffed version of Legacy, staring up at her in adoration. A little girl who might end up in those mines if Legacy didn't change the way things worked in this country. A little girl like Ink, or Hugo, or any one of the littles.

Then she remembered the mines. The groaning, the low ceilings and the narrow walls, the darkness, and the visions.

Legacy clenched her jaw. "Whatever I may have said in the past," she started again, "I stand before you today to say that I condemn Silla's initiatives in Minori. Those mines: they are dangerous. People are dying. Whole swaths of our country are being polluted, all to pull more metium from the mines, to enrich a few people who live in the city. There are better ways. There are better ways to address the poverty in this country."

While she talked, the crowd grew quiet. Then someone jostled someone else, more people moved, a tunnel opened. At the end of it, Silla. Standing straight in her elegant silks, looking directly at Legacy with her eyes so cold and absent they seemed to be holes bored in the paper mask of her face.

The silence hovered. After a few seconds, Legacy had the impulse to cough or clear her throat, just to hear something. Anything. But someone in the crowd beat her to it.

"Down with the high consul!" came the shout from high up in the stands.

Suddenly there was another rush: reporters, fans, children, adults. The tunnel closed; Silla was gone. For a moment, Legacy remembered

Van and desperately searched the crowds to see if she could find him. But the world was closing in on her. Everyone was trying to reach her.

Javi and Pippa attached themselves to her sides, swatting away hands and loudspeakers and pads and pencils. They escorted her over the net, down the walkway, through the locker room, and up the darkening cobblestone street to their hotel.

The noise from the street filtered up to their window all night. From behind the curtains, Legacy looked out.

There were shouts, protests, organized marches. She had caused them.

For a moment, Legacy allowed herself to feel proud. She had lit a match in her country.

CHAPTER TWENTY-TWO

THE FUNDAMENTALS

Legacy, Pippa, and Javi snuck out of the hotel early the next morning in disguise to avoid the crowds of reporters, and they were back in the orphanage by late afternoon. It was such a beautiful night in the forest that Hugo, Ink, and Jenni decided to turn the welcome-home feast they had planned into a picnic.

While Hugo put the last touches on the feast he'd been concocting, Legacy went up to the attic to gather old tapestries to lay out in a patchwork quilt in the garden. There, looking at Van's stacks of books, she thought about the way he'd recognized her. He'd seen her. Just as he always had, he'd known what she was trying to say before she said it out loud. She missed him. She hoped he was okay. Maybe, tomorrow, she'd see if there was some way she could send him word in the city. Let him know that he could come home, even if things had changed. Even if there was still so much unspoken between them.

For the time being, however, there were littles clamoring for her attention, and dishes to carry out from the kitchen. Hugo had outdone himself: there were truffles stacked as tall as towers on the picnic blanket Ink had spread out, and honey cakes that dripped with golden honey, and nipperberry jam, and soft wheels of cheese made of goat's milk, and some sort of soup that steamed in the cauldron. Ink was presiding as the master of ceremonies. Zaza, for reasons unknown, was wearing a hollowed-out loaf of bread as a crown and waving around a long fork like a wand. Hugo was imitating everything Javi did, Gus was in the baby carriage, and Legacy tried to run over to Zaza to take the fork and put it away safely, but she tripped on the basket of corn bread and fell face-first into a big soft wheel of fresh cheese.

There was uproarious laughter from the assembled littles. Legacy, not for the first time, thought about the fact that she was now champion of the Capari Open, and this was not how champions were supposed to be treated. But then Zaza kissed her, and Javi helped her up, and she thought: *Or perhaps this is exactly how champions are supposed to be treated.*

Grinning, she licked some of the cheese off her face, then grabbed a piece of corn bread and dipped it straight into the cauldron.

When she looked up, she saw Van letting himself in through the garden gate.

"Hi," he said.

Legacy stared.

He was wearing his old burlap shift instead of his scholar's gown, and his glasses sat crookedly on his nose.

"Hi," he said again, glancing around at the assembled company. Pippa and Javi were staring. Jenni was glaring. The littles had gone silent, as though they knew something was wrong and couldn't jump all over Van yet. Van straightened his glasses. "Before you say anything back, please—just know I'm more sorry than anyone has ever been sorry about anything. If I could blame Ancient Stringing Craft, I would. If I could say it was a double me up there, cheering for that . . . for that fake . . . I would. But it was just me. Stupid me—"

Legacy almost moved forward to hug him, then held herself back. Something in her was still hurt. She couldn't let it go so easily. Still, she gave him a smile. "It's okay, Van. I'm just happy to see you. I'm glad you're safe."

Van shook his head. "No. Don't let me off the hook so easily. I think—I think I got to the city and . . . I just wanted to be a new person. Not some poor orphan. Not a kid with a limp. Someone impressive. Someone important. A better version of me."

Legacy thought of the envy she'd felt when she'd watched False Legacy in that exhibition match. That version of herself that was unfazed by the pressure. Perfectly graceful. Always smiling. She hadn't just hated that other Legacy. She'd wanted to be her. She understood what Van was talking about.

"So when Silla summoned me, and started giving me gifts, like that pair of new glasses, and asking my opinion on economic decisions, I was—I was incredibly flattered," Van said. "I knew I shouldn't trust her, but still: I was flattered. And then she brought me your letter, the one asking me to write you a detailed description of you, because you were struggling to remember the person you'd been before you were a champion, and I thought: If Silla really wanted to harm Legacy, she wouldn't bring me this letter."

Legacy stared. "My letter? Asking you for a description—"

"The formula for a string double," Pippa breathed. "She needed someone close to Legacy to describe her."

Legacy smiled in spite of herself. "She must have intercepted all my other letters, all my real letters. And used the handwriting in those to forge this one."

Van smacked his forehead with the palm of his hand. "And I

bought it. Fool that I am, I bought it. And then you showed up. Or she showed up. And by then I was so lonely, and you hadn't written back to my letter, and I was so happy to see you, or her, I just didn't stop to think . . ."

He trailed off. His shoulders slumped. Once again, he pushed his broken glasses up on his nose.

Legacy smiled. "But, Van—you don't have to wear your old glasses."

He smiled ruefully. "I prefer them, honestly. The other ones didn't even have the right prescription. Half the time I couldn't see where I was going."

Legacy hugged her oldest friend in the world. Van hugged her back. Then all the littles piled on, and for some reason Pippa piled on also.

Javi and Jenni, however, hung back. Jenni was still glaring at him with suspicion. And, seeing that, Legacy felt her own flash of concern. She pulled away from the hug. If Silla had been capable of making a Legacy who fooled Van, why couldn't she make a Van to fool her?

"But wait a minute," she said. "Just—before you say anything else. How did you get here? You just . . . appeared out of nowhere."

Van blushed. "Well, besides getting bad glasses, the only real benefit of being Silla's pawn is . . . you get your own pyrus."

He turned, and Legacy looked beyond the garden wall. There was a sleek black pyrus nosing the gate.

Legacy gasped. "He's beautiful! What's his name?"

"Her name is Shelley," Van said. "And she loves kids."

"Well, that's good!" Legacy laughed.

"It—it *is* good, because . . . well, I want to come back. I'd have gotten here sooner, but I had to go back and withdraw from school and, well, borrow Shelley for the time being. And"—he glanced at Jenni, who was still eyeing him suspiciously—"I know I can't just show up," Van said, "and assume the right to live here again. I know it'll take a long time to earn your trust. And your father's trust, too. But I think I can, and I'm ready to help out more with the littles, and that'll give you more time to train, and to—"

Something in Legacy's face must have stopped him.

"What?" he said. "What is it?"

Legacy looked at her other friends. "Can you guys take this for a minute?" she said, gesturing at the picnic and the littles who had already coated Shelley in honey. Pippa nodded. Javi and Jenni helped Hugo start to clear away the dishes. And Legacy led Van into the forest. Because she didn't know what to say, she moved down the path in silence to the scissor grass clearing where Legacy's father's arch still stood.

When she told him what had happened, Van cried. Legacy didn't. She comforted her friend. His glasses fogged up twice. He wiped them off on the hem of his old burlap.

Finally, once his shoulders had stopped shaking, they headed back. Shoulder to shoulder, they walked down the old forest path, a path they had walked together many, many times.

Even after everything, Legacy felt like herself again in Van's presence. Walking with him on the soft moss, under the boughs of the cyca-press. She smiled a little sadly to herself, thinking of one of Javi's refrains about process: it's all about the fundamentals. The fundamental drills, and the fundamental friends: that's what leads you back to yourself.

Or so Legacy thought, walking with Van down the path in the forest. When they got back to the garden, Gus and Shelley were galloping in circles, chasing each other. It was a happy sight. Pippa and Javi were restraining hooting littles from running out and trying to leap on the pyruses as they played. Zaza had whipped cream in her hair; a new little with wide black eyes was dipping a cycapress twig into the honey.

After everyone had eaten their fill, they relaxed and played on the blankets while the sun set low over the olive groves. The sky was streaked with tangerine. Then it was navy blue. Then it was black, and the last of the blue wazoons had gone to sleep in the canopies of the cherish trees, and the owls were starting to call, and the lightning bugs rose and fell all around them.

"You know," Van said as the first littles started to nod off on a blanket. "When I went back to the city this morning, I checked the tapestry. It's blurry. Silla's image, I mean: its outlines have changed. Now they're unclear. Not just for a few minutes. Things must be really changing. Her face, on the tapestry, isn't recognizable."

Legacy listened, remembering the last tournament she had won. The nationals, when she beat Gia, and Silla's image on the tapestry had briefly turned blurry, then sharpened again.

"It's what everyone in the city is talking about," Van said. "A real referendum. It hasn't happened since the Great Fire. But now people are changing their mind about Silla. And if her image stays blurred, she'll have to share power—"

Jenni interrupted him. "That means the senators will get an equal vote. Our senator, the senator from Minori: she'll get to vote against building new mines."

Pippa chimed in. "And the senator from Cora can vote for funds to fight forest fires—"

Javi was grinning at her. "And it's all because of you, Leg. Because of what you did at Capari."

"It's because of *us*," Legacy said. "And because of everyone in the country—"

"But yeah, also us," Javi said.

"My meditation techniques," Pippa said, grinning slyly.

"Reps and sweat," Javi said, pretending to be angry.

Jenni was laughing. "Not to mention playing *me*—"

Legacy laughed along with her friends. They kept up the fake bickering, and she turned her attention to the stars that seemed to be caught in the branches of the newly planted nipperberry tree.

Then Legacy realized what they actually were: dewdrops, caught in a cobweb.

They reminded her of the cobwebs in the old gym they'd found in the forest. Now she imagined dusting them away. Washing the cycapress wood floors until they gleamed. Fixing up the old courts. Figuring out what they were: the one with the weird sucking sand, the one with the high net. And filling them with children from the provinces.

It was what her parents had wanted. Her mother, Amata, who left before Legacy really knew her. And her father, who loved this forest. He was gone now, but somehow Legacy still felt his presence. She watched the dewy little web glisten in the night. And she looked beyond it, to the Forest of Cora, lately so full of life. Now, in the darkness, the lush leaves on the cherish trees whispered together. Their murmuring sounded like her father's voice.

A few Herman's Wingfeathers cooed. The lightning bugs rose and fell. The white talon moths winged their way through the darkness. The forest was finally coming back to life, all these years after the fire.

Legacy smiled. She glanced around at the littles, curled up on the blanket with their heads on Gus's belly and their toes on Shelley's. She looked at her friends, still happily chattering.

This, she thought, *is where I belong.*

How she wished her father were here to share this moment with her. Legacy closed her eyes. She could see him, propped up in his bed: You choose goodness, he had said.

Legacy smiled. *This*, she thought, *is where I choose to belong.*

This is who I choose to be.

She took a deep breath, a breath like Pippa had taught her. She felt herself settling into her body. *These*, she thought, *are my fundamentals.*

These are my friends.

This is my forest.

I am Legacy Petrin. I am my father's daughter, and I am a champion.

THE MAMBA & MAMBACITA SPORTS FOUNDATION

is a nonprofit organization that was founded in loving memory of Kobe and Gianna "Gigi" Bryant and is dedicated to creating positive impact for underserved athletes and young women in sports.

To help continue Kobe's and Gigi's legacies, please visit MambaAndMambacita.org.

KOBE BRYANT was an Academy Award winner, a *New York Times* best-selling author, and the CEO of Granity Studios, a multimedia content creation company. He was also a five-time NBA champion, two-time NBA Finals MVP, NBA MVP, and two-time Olympic gold medalist. Above all else, he was a loving husband and a doting father to four girls. In everything he built, Kobe was driven to teach the next generation how to reach their full potential. He believed in the beauty of the process, in the strength that comes from inner magic, and in achieving the impossible. His legacy continues today.

ANNIE MATTHEW is a novelist and a poet. In a former life, she was a professional athlete. She now lives in Iowa with her gray furry dog, Gus.

GRANITY STUDIOS, LLC
GRANITYSTUDIOS.COM

Copyright © 2021 by Granity Studios, LLC

Library of Congress Control Number: 2021935352
ISBN (hardcover): 9781949520194
ISBN (ebook): 9781949520200

Printed in the United States of America
1 3 5 7 9 10 8 6 4 2

Book design by Karina Granda
Cover illustration by Sunya Mara
Type design by Seb Lester
Art direction by Sharanya Durvasula
Endpaper art by Jana Heidersdorf